"Let's go into d, watching Tia alm   a step up from Je   ed Elizabeth silently   wn opposite her—Elizabeth on the   ove seat.

Tia cleared her throat, deciding to jump right in. "Okay, first of all, I want to make sure that you know that absolutely nothing happened." She waited for some kind of relief to cross Elizabeth's features, but instead the girl's eyes flashed.

"Nice, Tia," she scoffed. "Why don't you try the truth?"

"What?" Tia blurted out. She couldn't help it. There wasn't a coherent thought in her head.

"Conner already told me you guys kissed," Elizabeth informed her, crossing her arms.

"He—" Tia snapped her mouth shut before she could say something stupid. But her mind was reeling. He'd told her. How could he do that? No possible good could come of it. And for some reason, her heart felt like it had just been pierced with an arrow. If he'd told Elizabeth, that meant it wasn't worth keeping a secret to him, which meant it meant nothing.

Nothing at all.

Don't miss any of the books in SWEET VALLEY HIGH
SENIOR YEAR, an exciting series from Bantam Books!

Visit the Official Sweet Valley Web Site on the Internet at:

http://www.sweetvalley.com

Francine Pascal's SVH senioryear

Backstabber

CREATED BY
FRANCINE PASCAL

BANTAM BOOKS
NEW YORK • TORONTO • LONDON • SYDNEY • AUCKLAND

RL: 6, AGES 012 AND UP

BACKSTABBER
A Bantam Book / May 2000

Sweet Valley High® is a registered trademark of Francine Pascal.
Conceived by Francine Pascal.
Cover photography by Michael Segal.

Produced by 17th Street Productions, Inc.
33 West 17th Street
New York, NY 10011.

ISBN: 0-553-49316-7

Visit us on the Web! www.randomhouse.com/teens

Published simultaneously in the United States and Canada

Bantam Books is an imprint of Random House Children's Books, a
division of Random House, Inc. BANTAM BOOKS and the rooster
colophon are registered trademarks of Random House, Inc. Bantam Books,
1540 Broadway, New York, New York 10036.

PRINTED IN THE UNITED STATES OF AMERICA

OPM   0 9 8 7 6 5 4 3 2 1

To Keely Alexandra Schafer

Elizabeth Wakefield

Did I miss something?

Because the last time I checked, Tia was my friend, and Conner was <u>my</u> boyfriend. Still, I know what I saw, and that means . . .

That means—

God, I don't even want to think about it.

It's time I stopped ignoring the obvious. I've been making excuses for them spending so much time together for too long. It's time for me to get real.

Conner's cheating on me.

And so is Tia.

Conner McDermott

Leave it to Liz to get all hysterical before she even knows what's going on. I mean, it's not like Tia and I were doing <u>anything</u>.

We just fell asleep watching TV . . . in her bed.

And we kissed <u>once.</u>

Okay, twice.

TIA RAMIREZ

BACKSTABBERS ARE THE LOWEST OF THE LOW.

I REMEMBER ONCE WHEN MY BROTHER RICKY WAS THIRTEEN, THERE WAS THIS GIRL WHO LIKED HIM. SHE USED TO CALL HIM EVERY NIGHT, AND HE'D BE ON THE PHONE WITH HER FOR, LIKE, HOURS AT A TIME, ACTING REALLY NICE AND EVERYTHING. BUT THEN HE'D GET TOGETHER WITH HIS FRIENDS, WHO ALWAYS MADE FUN OF HER FOR CALLING, AND HE'D JOIN RIGHT IN. I HEARD HIM ONCE, AND I GOT SO MAD THAT I MADE ALL HIS FRIENDS GO HOME. THEN I SAT HIM DOWN AND TOLD HIM THAT LEADING A GIRL ON THAT WAY WAS ONE OF THE WORST THINGS HE COULD EVER DO AND THAT HE EITHER NEEDED TO BE UP FRONT WITH

HER AND TELL HER TO STOP CALLING OR TELL HIS FRIENDS TO STOP WHEN THEY STARTED DISSING HER. SO HE DID.

THE NEXT TIME HIS BUDDIES CAME OVER, HE TOLD THEM HE ACTUALLY THOUGHT SHE WAS PRETTY COOL, AND THAT WAS THE END OF IT. I WAS SO PROUD OF HIM, I COULD HAVE KISSED HIM RIGHT THERE, BUT I KNEW IT WOULD HAVE TOTALLY EMBARRASSED HIM, SO I DIDN'T. ANYWAY, MY POINT IS, I'VE ALWAYS HATED PEOPLE WHO WERE DISHONEST AND TWO-FACED.

THE PROBLEM?

LATELY I'VE BECOME ONE OF THOSE PEOPLE I HATE.

Andy Marsden

It's funny. You grow up with all of these images of couples. Your mom and dad, your friends' parents, Superman and Lois Lane. And you always just figure that sooner or later, you'll end up as somebody's "better half," you know? So I guess I always just assumed that someday I'd meet a girl, get married, buy a house, have kids, yada, yada, yada—the whole deal.

But now I'm not so sure.

I mean, what if I'm just one of those people who's destined to go through life alone? What if there's no one out there for me?

Or what if there is, but it's not a girl? I don't know if I could handle that.

I guess I should just be happy that I have good friends like Tia and Conner to talk to. I mean, when you think about it, what more does anyone really need anyway?

Jessica Wakefield

My sister's crying her eyes out (again), and it's all because of Conner (again).

I can't believe Tia. Conner, I can believe, but Tia?

I guess it just goes to show there's no getting around the first rule of Romance 101:

Single guys and girls <u>cannot</u> be just friends.

It may start out that way, sure, but sooner or later, someone wants more and something's bound to happen. Look at Maria and Ken. Liz and Conner. And now Tia and Conner. Of course, there are occasional exceptions. Like me and Jeremy. That's totally platonic. Or Andy and . . . anyone.

I'm not sure Andy even has hormones.

But that's a topic for another time.

My advice? If a guy and a girl claim they're just friends, wait a week and ask again. They'll probably be so busy playing tonsil hockey, they won't be able to answer.

CHAPTER
Once Is Enough

1

"Come on, Liz! I know you're standing right there," Conner yelled from the other side of the door. Elizabeth stood as silently as possible in the foyer of her house on Calico Drive.

I can't deal with this, she told herself, squeezing her eyes shut. If she didn't answer, maybe he would just give up and leave. But five seconds later the pounding came again.

"Liz, open the door. I have to talk to you." Even through two inches of solid oak Conner's voice sounded urgent, and every blow of his fist shook the large wooden door.

"Just go away," Elizabeth whispered. "I don't want to see you." She knew he couldn't hear her, but she didn't have the energy to say it any louder. She squeezed her eyes shut even tighter, but it was no use. She couldn't shake the image of Conner and Tia in bed together. "Oh God," she muttered when he stopped banging again, wishing she could just disappear.

At that moment Jessica returned from the bath-

1

room, holding a box of tissues. She pulled one out and offered it to her sister.

"Thanks," Elizabeth murmured, trying to hold in the tears. She wiped her eyes and nose while staring at the door. When Conner suddenly started beating on it again, Elizabeth jumped.

"He's lucky Mom and Dad aren't around," Jessica said. "Dad would kill him for thrashing on the new door like that." She paused and examined Elizabeth's expression. "Actually, forget Dad. Mom would kill him first if she could see your face." Elizabeth stared blankly at her sister. The realization that she looked as horrible as she felt wasn't exactly comforting.

Jessica put her arm around her twin. "Look— why don't you just go upstairs? I'll get rid of him," she said, nodding toward the door. "I'd kind of like to tell him where to go right now."

Elizabeth tried to smile, but she couldn't pull it off. Jessica was right to hate him, but it still hurt. When had Conner gone from being the guy she loved to the hideous jerk on the other side of the door?

Oh, right. The second he jumped in bed with Tia. Elizabeth leaned into her sister's shoulder and let the tears flow freely. Now that she wasn't trying to contain them, her sobs came out in a series of high-pitched gasps, and her breathing bordered on hyperventilation. She felt Jessica's arm tighten around her.

"Forget Mom and Dad. *I* could kill him," Jessica spat. She separated herself from her sister and took a step toward the door, but Elizabeth held her back.

"Don't," Elizabeth said, forcing herself to take a deep breath. Jessica looked on as Elizabeth composed herself, and after a moment Elizabeth actually felt like she might have the crying under control. *Probably because my tear ducts have dried out,* she thought. She straightened up and reached for another tissue, doing what she could to clean up her face as Jessica fed her one Kleenex after another.

"Really, Liz. Trust me," Jessica said, her face taut with anger. "If you let me take care of *lover boy* out there for you, he won't be coming back anytime soon. At least not without a severe limp."

"Thanks," Elizabeth said wearily, dabbing at her eyes one last time. "But I should probably do it." She balled up her wad of tissues and tossed them into the small garbage can beneath her mother's rolltop desk.

"Come on, Liz! Open up," Conner yelled.

The door bowed beneath another round of Conner's pummeling. Elizabeth turned to her sister. "So do I look totally messed up or what?" she asked.

"You look fine," Jessica answered, clearing a strand of blond hair from Elizabeth's face. Jessica's hand was gentle enough, but her eyes were fiercely protective. "Okay, if you're going to do this, I might as well get to HOJ." She glanced at the shaking door.

"I'll go out the back. Now, give him hell—and don't let him talk his way out of it. He's an idiot, and he did an idiot thing—don't let him forget it."

Elizabeth nodded. "I won't," she said, surprised at how clear her voice sounded. She would have thanked Jessica for being so supportive, but she knew that even the smallest show of emotion would immediately reduce her to tears again, and that wasn't what she wanted. When she faced Conner, it would be obvious that she was hurt and upset, but she wanted him to know she was angry. Jessica was right. Conner *was* an idiot. She just hoped she could remember that when he was standing only two inches away.

"I'll see you later," Jessica said, throwing her one last sympathetic glance before heading for the kitchen.

"Liz, just let me in, dammit! I can explain," Conner yelled.

Elizabeth took a last deep breath. *I can do this,* she told herself, walking to the door. She swung it open in one quick motion, catching Conner's arm in midknock. The blue sky over his head looked surreal in contrast with his clenched fist and Elizabeth's dark mood.

"Liz," he said quietly, obviously taken by surprise. His intense green eyes scanned her up and down, causing Elizabeth to shiver despite the heat wafting in through the open door. *He even looks good when I hate him,* she thought, noticing that the tensed muscles along his neck

4

and shoulders only seemed to make him sexier.

But as he took in her face, he seemed to relax a little, his features softening as he drew back, proving that Jessica had been overly generous when she said Elizabeth looked fine. "Are you okay?" he asked, all concern.

Elizabeth snorted. "Oh, yeah, fine. I'm having a great morning. How about you?"

Conner rolled his eyes, the tension returning to his face. "Look, it's not what you think. You're getting yourself all worked up over nothing."

"Nothing?" Elizabeth exclaimed, widening her eyes. "That's funny. Because I was just over at Tia's, and she was in bed with this guy who looked exactly like you." Conner opened his mouth, but Elizabeth cut him off. "Oh, wait! Don't tell me. You have a twin too, right?"

Conner shook his head and stared down at his feet. Elizabeth couldn't help noticing how tired he looked, but she wasn't about to let herself feel sorry for him. He was the one who screwed up, not her.

"You're jumping to conclusions, Liz," he said.

"Really? I find you in bed with your best friend— or whatever she is—and you think I'm jumping to conclusions?" Elizabeth crossed her arms over her chest. "Tell me, what other conclusions are there?"

Sighing heavily, Conner looked directly into her eyes. "I know how it looked," he said, "but nothing happened."

Elizabeth's heart jumped. Somewhere in the back of her mind there was a glimmer of hope, but she was too scared to trust it.

"Really?" she asked, her voice barely above a whisper. Conner blinked once and dropped his gaze, staring down at the brick doorstep, and immediately Elizabeth felt like she had been shot straight through the heart. She brought her hand to her stomach, unable to breathe.

"We kissed," Conner said quietly before raising his eyes to hers once again. "But that was it. I swear."

His green eyes were pleading with her, and Elizabeth had heard the conviction in his voice, but it didn't matter. *They kissed* was echoing through her brain too fast for anything else to get in. It was too much to handle.

With one hard push she slammed the door in his face.

"Elizabeth!" Conner called, but Elizabeth could barely hear him.

They kissed, she thought, pressing her back against the door and sinking slowly to the floor. *And he has the nerve to say 'that was it'?* She buried her head in her hands.

Well, that was enough.

"Home, sweet home," Jeremy Aames murmured as he grasped the cool metal door handle at House of Java.

He smiled slightly, chiding his silliness as he walked inside. During the last few months, when his home life had been beyond stressful, House of Java had become a sort of safe haven for him—a place where he always felt like he had at least a measure of control over what happened. And even now that his family's finances and living arrangements had improved, Jeremy still felt a strange sense of relief every time he showed up for work.

I bet there aren't too many people who can say that about their jobs, he thought as the familiar scent of freshly ground coffee enveloped him.

"Hey, Jeremy," said Ally Scott, the shop's manager, glancing over from behind the counter. "Early as always."

Jeremy smirked and pulled off his blue-and-gold Big Mesa varsity jacket. "Can't help it," he said. "I think I'm wired wrong." He strolled over to the counter and leaned on one of the stools. "I'm not the first one, am I?"

"No. Daniel's in the back," Ally said, scrubbing intently at a coffee stain on the green countertop. "Who cleaned this place up last night, the Tasmanian devil?" she asked with exasperation.

"I think Corey closed," Jeremy said. He ran a hand through his short, brown hair and tried not to grin.

"Oh." Ally didn't look at all surprised. Corey was her younger, more obnoxious sister who never bothered to break a sweat doing anything. "Shocker."

"Need help?" Jeremy asked.

Ally pushed a few strands of straight brown hair off her face and sighed. "No, I got it," she said, tossing the rag she was working with into the sink. "We need to talk before the staff meeting starts anyway."

Jeremy felt his stomach tighten. *Uh-oh. In work or relationships those are the last words you ever want to hear,* he thought, swallowing hard.

The bells at the door jangled, and Jeremy was suddenly so tense, he almost jumped. Suzanne and Nancy, two older women who worked day shifts, walked in and headed straight for the back, where meetings were usually held.

"Hey, guys!" Suzanne called. Ally said hello back, but Jeremy just lifted his chin.

"So, what's up?" he asked Ally in a low voice as soon as the two women were settled and gabbing on a couch near the wall. Logically he knew Ally couldn't have anything terrible to say. But he also knew that "we need to talk" rarely led to anything good.

Ally leaned her elbows on the counter and looked him in the eye. "I just wanted to give you a heads up," she said. "I promoted Jessica to assistant manager last night, and I plan to announce it at the meeting this morning."

Jeremy drew back as though she had just slapped him across the face. He couldn't possibly have heard right. Jeremy had *trained* Jessica. And she'd only been working at HOJ half as long as he had. Where was this coming from?

Jeremy tried for an enthusiastic reaction. "Um . . . that's great," he managed, sounding confused. Ally studied his expression, and he knew she was waiting for more, but he wasn't sure what to say. She was, after all, his boss.

"Is that it?" she asked, one hand on her hip. "You're not even going to ask me *why* I promoted Jessica and not you?"

Jeremy squirmed in his seat, running his hand over his hair again. He'd worked for Ally for almost a year now, but sometimes her bluntness still threw him.

"Well . . . now that you mention it . . . ," he said finally, allowing his voice to trail off.

"I figured you might be upset," Ally said, nodding. She scratched at the counter with her thumbnail, sending a crumb flying to the floor. "That's why I wanted to tell you first."

Jeremy shrugged, going for the casual thing. "Well, I wouldn't exactly say I'm 'upset,' but yeah, I am a little confused. I mean . . . did I do something wrong?"

Ally chuckled, which caused Jeremy's cheeks to flare up. He didn't think he was being particularly funny.

"I'm sorry," she told him, shaking her head. "If anything, you did too much *right.*" Jeremy narrowed his eyes. Now he was *really* confused. "Look," Ally continued, standing up straight with both hands flat on the counter. "You're a great employee—responsible, prompt, conscientious, hardworking. You know all that. It's just that I think it's time you took a little break."

"You're kidding me," Jeremy said with an incredulous chuckle. Then his heart slammed against his rib cage. "Wait a minute—you're not *firing* me, are you?"

Ally laughed again, louder this time. Jeremy clenched his jaw and shoved his hands into the pockets of his khakis.

"No, I'm not firing you," Ally insisted. "But this is exactly what I'm talking about," she added, pointing a finger at him. Jeremy felt his chest tighten as he crossed his arms over it.

"What?" he demanded. By now every muscle in his body was tensed—even his ears were getting red.

"This," she answered calmly, looking him up and down. "Jeremy, I like to think that we're friends, right?"

Jeremy nodded mutely.

"Well, as your friend, I have to tell you," Ally continued, "you've been so high-strung lately, I'm afraid if I pile any more responsibility on you, you'll explode."

Jeremy eyed her skeptically. Interesting excuse. Making herself look like the good guy.

"Listen," Ally continued, "you're the only worker I have who's always here twenty minutes early and willing to stay two hours late—which is great, and I've appreciated it, but it makes me wonder. . . . Do you have a life outside of work? Aside from football and homework, I mean?"

Jeremy opened his mouth, ready to let her have it, but he was stumped. *Oh, come on,* he told himself, shifting his gaze to the ceiling, *that was a major insult.* He had to have a comeback. But the harder he tried to come up with something, the emptier his mind seemed. "What's wrong with football and homework?" he asked finally.

Ally shook her head. "Nothing. All I know is, a high-school senior who pours coffee for a few hours a week should *not* be as stressed out about life as you are."

"I'm not stressed out," Jeremy insisted automatically, but even as he tried to defend himself, he could feel his pulse rapidly approaching warp speed.

Okay, so he was having an over-the-top reaction to this news. And things had been crazy lately with midterms, college applications, his dad's latest physical, baby-sitting for his sisters, the upcoming play-offs, breaking up with Jessica. . . .

Maybe he *was* just a walking stress ball. Jeremy was about to concede as much when the door opened again. This time a whole crowd walked in.

"Here comes the rest of the crew," Ally said, leaning

toward him. "If you want to talk about this some more, I'll be in my office for a while after the meeting."

"Okay," Jeremy said, gathering up his jacket. He still wasn't sure how he felt about this whole thing, but his confusion went on the back burner when he turned around and spotted a stranger in the little group of employees. A very attractive stranger.

"Hi, Jade," Ally said, waving the new girl over. "I'm glad you could make it on such short notice."

Jade. What a cool name. Her thick, shoulder-length, black hair framed her face perfectly, accentuating her dark eyes and smooth lips. She was the most gorgeous girl he'd seen since he first laid eyes on Jessica Wakefield.

"Hey," Jeremy said, nodding slightly as she approached the counter.

"Hey, yourself," she answered, almost knocking him over with her boldness. She didn't blink and look away like most girls did when they were being stared at. She stared back. And when she brushed past him to speak to Ally, he distinctly felt his heart skip.

Jeremy's palms started to sweat. It had been a while since he'd had that feeling. He moved over a little so that Jade and Ally could talk, but instead of mingling with any of his coworkers, Jeremy stayed close to the counter and listened in on their conversation. They started talking about hours, dress codes, minimum wage.

So he was going to be working with her. Interesting . . .

Maybe it really was time for Jeremy Aames to think about something other than football and homework.

"Girls suck," Conner muttered under his breath, slamming his car door violently. As he walked up the driveway toward his house, he kicked the small pebbles beneath his feet, leaving a chalky white cloud in his wake.

He took the steps two at a time and whipped open the screen door, gratified by the crash it made as it bounced against the wall and then slammed shut again. But he knew it was going to take a lot more than banging a few doors around to get a grip on his rage.

"Hey! Careful with that!" Mrs. Sandborn yelled.

Conner froze in the hallway, clenching his fists. Now was really not the time to deal with his new "involved" mother.

"It's about time you came home," she said, coming to the door that opened up into the foyer from the kitchen. Her arms were folded firmly across her chest. "I've been waiting. All night." Conner eyeballed his mother, trying to determine how much she knew. Her eyes betrayed nothing.

Conner exhaled slowly, staring at the ceiling. "Well, now you can stop waiting."

"Don't you take that tone with me," his mother said crisply. She unbuttoned the cuffs of her mint-colored blouse and rolled them up methodically. "I just got off the phone with Mrs. Ramirez. You have some explaining to do."

This is just great, Conner thought, pressing his eyes closed. He clenched his jaw and ordered himself to take a deep breath.

"Look," he said, barely parting his lips. "I don't need this right now." Mrs. Sandborn stared at him. Conner couldn't help noticing that she too seemed to be regulating her breathing.

"None of us needs this right now," she said slowly. "But here we are." She curved one side of her mouth ironically, and Conner felt his heart pounding inside his chest. For every second he stood there silently—without yelling, without hitting something—his heartbeat grew heavier and harder until finally he felt like he was ready to explode.

"We'll talk later when you've calmed down," she said finally, her shoulders slumping just a bit. "Right now I have to go out." She disappeared into the kitchen, and moments later Conner heard the back door close.

"Dammit!" Conner exploded, punching the doorjamb and causing a mirror on the wall to rattle. Now that he was alone, there was no containing the rage. He stormed into the living room, snatched his guitar case off the sofa, and stalked outside. Using

14

his free hand, he grasped the garage door handle and sent it up so quickly, it almost bounced back down. Within thirty seconds his guitar and amp were plugged into one of the dusty old outlets, but as much as he wanted to let loose, all Conner could do was watch his hand hover above the strings.

"Such an idiot!" he yelled, not sure at the moment whether he was talking about himself or his mother. He kicked the garage door so hard, the wood splintered. He moved on to the next panel.

That's for being such a moron, his internal voice screamed as he kicked the door again. *And that's for Liz's attitude!* Conner released another swift kick into the rattling wood panels. *And that one's for Tia—just for existing!* He turned and focused on a cluttered shelf piled with old toys, cans of nails and screws, and miscellaneous tools. Instantly Conner flew to the rear of the garage and cleared the shelf with his arm in one sweeping movement. Then, amidst the cacophony of falling metal, he fell to his knees, his chest heaving as he exhaled in forceful bursts.

After a few minutes his breathing returned to normal, although he could still feel the dull pounding of his heart.

"Well, that was good," he muttered sarcastically, snorting. He was acting like a psycho. He was about to stand when he noticed his knee was wet.

"What the—?" He rubbed at the dark spot with his

fingers and then lifted his hand just below his nose. The scent stung his nostrils, and he pulled back slightly.

No way, he thought, thumbing through the debris, but sure enough, there was the broken glass to confirm his suspicion. He picked up a glistening piece that was still clinging to a white label.

"Wild Turkey," he sneered, tossing the shard of glass at the wall. The idea of his mother hiding extra liquor around the house made his stomach turn. Especially after he and Megan had spent so much time ridding the house of alcohol so it would be clean when Mrs. Sandborn got back from rehab.

No one ever thought to check the garage. Conner laughed bitterly at the absurdity of it all. The curse of the alcoholic. Plenty of booze, but who was sober enough to remember where it was hidden? Conner turned to the opposite end of the garage and narrowed his eyes. Or how *much* of it was hidden.

Conner began searching the other shelves that lined the room, and within a minute he found a bottle of Jack Daniels whiskey. *Man, she was really sick,* he thought. *Probably still is.* Conner pulled out the plastic-topped cork and tilted the bottle over the floor drain.

"Sorry, Jack," he said, watching as the brown liquid trickled out, its acrid smell wafting up from the ground. It was half gone when Conner righted the bottle and lifted it to his nose slowly, inhaling the aroma. The sharp smell made him blink, but somehow it also made him salivate.

Just then the side door creaked open and Megan stuck her head in tentatively. "Conner, I—" Megan's green eyes widened beneath the fringe of her strawberry blond bangs. "What are you doing?"

Conner rolled his eyes. "It's *Mom's*. I found it out here, and I was just dumping it out."

Megan's eyes flitted to the puddle around the drain. "Oh, I'm sorry, I just . . . when I saw the bottle . . ." She moistened her lips and swallowed hard. "Here," she said, taking a step into the garage. "I'll help you."

"Don't bother," Conner barked. "Just go, okay?" He saw the way Megan flinched at the sound of his voice, but he didn't care. He was so sick of needy females. "Can't I get any privacy around here?"

Megan's eyes hardened. "Fine," she said abruptly, setting her jaw forward. "Excuse me for caring." Then she turned on her heel and walked out.

Once again Conner felt his heart bouncing like a racquetball ricocheting through his torso. He glanced down at the bottle in his hand.

Just one sip, he thought. *It'll calm my nerves. Then I can think things through. Think about Liz . . . think about Tia.* He brought the bottle to his lips and swallowed quickly, feeling the whiskey burn as it coated his throat. After coughing slightly, he caught his breath and took another drink.

You're just like your mother, McDermott, the cynical voice inside his head insisted.

"Hardly," Conner muttered before he tilted the

17

bottle back again. After all, when his mother drank, she lost control. "I'm always in control," Conner said. "There's a difference."

Jessica's heart was skipping excitedly as she entered House of Java. The place was already crowded with employees, and there was no containing her nervousness as she glanced around the room. She smoothed her black shorts over her thighs and reminded herself to stay calm. She didn't want anyone to feel like she was rubbing her promotion in their face.

Anyone named Jeremy anyway.

Jessica took a deep breath when she saw him leaning against the counter, chatting with a few other HOJ-ers. As always, he looked perfect even though it was ridiculously early in the morning. And he was smiling, oblivious to the fact that Jessica had basically usurped him. Jeremy was the only one of her coworkers who might be upset by the news that she was going to be an assistant manager. Everyone else was either younger or newer or would never want the job. But Jeremy lived for this kind of stuff.

He was like the poster boy for overachievers.

Maybe I should tell him about it in advance, she thought. *Soften the blow.*

She cleared her throat and stepped toward the counter, wondering how she was going to pull him away with all these people around.

"Hey, Jess," Daniel said as she approached. "Ready for the big meeting?" He winked, and Jessica realized he already knew she was being promoted. Ally had probably clued him in before she had even mentioned it to Jessica.

"Oh . . . yeah," she said nervously.

She glanced over at Jeremy, but there was someone standing between them. The girl had her back to Jessica, but Jessica would recognize that perfect black shoulder-length bob anywhere.

"Jade?" Jessica said, her brows raised. Instantly her friend whirled around, her sharply angled hair bouncing from side to side.

"Hey, Jess," she said casually, as if it weren't at all odd for her to be at House of Java before opening on a Saturday morning. "I was wondering when you were going to show up."

Jeremy straightened up, his forehead creasing. "You two know each other?" he asked.

"Yeah," Jessica answered matter-of-factly. Then Jeremy's phrasing hit her. "Do *you two* know each other?" she asked, puzzled. How would Jade know Jeremy? And why would she be coming to a staff meeting with him? A sudden tightness across Jessica's chest took her by surprise.

"Actually we just met," Jeremy answered, smiling. "Jade's our newest employee."

"Really?" Jessica asked Jade, feeling strangely relieved. "What happened to First and Ten?"

Jade rolled her eyes. "I couldn't take that place anymore. It was always so loud, and the drunks kept hitting on me."

"Yeah," Jessica said with a chuckle. "I don't know how Maria does it. It never struck me as a very fun place to work. At least here the people are sober— they're just overcaffeinated."

"Hyper I can handle," Jade stated. Jeremy laughed, and Jessica shot him a glance. Was Jade's comment really laugh worthy? Jeremy blushed and glanced away. Oookay.

"When did you get hired?" Jessica asked, quickly returning her attention to Jade. Her heart was hammering again, and she suddenly realized it no longer had anything to do with nerves. "I was in here yesterday afternoon, talking to Ally, and she didn't say anything about it."

"That's because she hadn't hired me yet," Jade said, leaning back and propping her arms up on the counter. "I filled out an application a while ago," she explained. "Then Ally finally called me last night at, like, nine o'clock. She said if I could make it to the staff meeting this morning, I could have the job."

Jeremy laughed and crossed his arms over his middle. "Sounds like Ally."

"Yeah, it does," Jessica said, trying to ignore the fact that Jeremy was continually laughing for no apparent reason. "She's kind of . . . abrupt."

Jade shook her head, letting her hair all fall to

one side. "Oh, well. Better abrupt than boring," she said with a slight shrug.

"I guess," Jessica said. She looked at Jeremy, but he was just grinning foolishly. Before she could smack him upside the head, Ally emerged from the back room.

"All right, we're ready to start," she called out. An immediate hush fell over the room. "I want to make this quick so the morning shift can clean up some more before we open." Everyone nodded, but Ally didn't pause long enough to take note. "Okay, first order of business. I'm promoting Jessica to assistant manager effective immediately."

Jessica's heart hit the floor. There was that abruptness again. There was a smattering of applause, and Jessica looked around to see how everyone was really taking the news. Daniel gave her a quick thumbs-up, but he'd already known. Corey was picking a piece of dirt out from under her fingernails.

Then Jessica did what she knew she was avoiding and glanced at Jeremy.

Her heart sank all over again. His face said it all. And he was hurt.

"Congratulations," he said, forcing a smile. Then he quickly looked away, as if there was something fascinating about the brick wall on the other side of the room.

Maybe being a manager wasn't going to be as cool as she'd thought.

Just then Jade leaned closer and nudged Jessica's upper arm. "You must be *very* proud," she whispered. "Maybe you can make a career out of pouring coffee," she added with a slight smirk.

"Oh, shut up," Jessica murmured, giggling quietly at Jade's familiar sarcasm.

She looked at Jeremy's rigid shoulders and sighed. It was a good thing Jade had been hired when she was.

Something told Jessica she was going to be needing a new friend around HOJ.

TIA RAMIREZ

REASONS I SHOULD WAIT A
DAY TO TALK TO LIZ:

I NEED TO GIVE CONNER A
SHOT AT CLEARING THINGS UP
BEFORE I GO GETTING IN THE
MIDDLE—AGAIN.

IF I WAIT TWENTY-FOUR HOURS,
SHE MAY NOT SHOOT ON SIGHT.

LIZ COULD PROBABLY USE A
DAY TO DECOMPRESS AND GET
OVER THE IMAGE OF ME AND
CONNER IN BED TOGETHER—NOT
THAT WE WERE REALLY
TOGETHER. WE WEREN'T. AT
LEAST, I DON'T THINK WE WERE.

I COULD USE A DAY TO GET
OVER THE IMAGE OF ME AND
CONNER IN BED TOGETHER. I
MEAN, CONNER IS MY FRIEND—
MY BEST FRIEND, AND I'VE
NEVER THOUGHT OF HIM AS

ANYTHING ELSE. UNTIL NOW. NOT THAT I'M ACTUALLY THINKING OF HIM AS, LIKE, A BOYFRIEND OR SOMETHING BECAUSE HE'S NOT. I MEAN, OBVIOUSLY HE CAN'T BE BECAUSE OF LIZ, BUT EVEN IF LIZ WEREN'T IN THE PICTURE, WE STILL COULDN'T BE A COUPLE BECAUSE . . . WELL, WE JUST COULDN'T.

IF ONLY ANGEL HADN'T LEFT. NOT THAT I THINK I BELONG WITH ANGEL OR ANYTHING, BUT IT'S LIKE, BEFORE, THERE WAS ALWAYS ANGEL AND CONNER WAS . . . JUST CONNER. BUT ALL OF A SUDDEN I CAN'T SEEM TO THINK OF HIM AS JUST CONNER ANYMORE. WHEN HE KISSED ME THIS MORNING, IT WAS LIKE SOMETHING CHANGED. I DON'T KNOW WHAT, BUT—IT'S TOO WEIRD TO EVEN THINK ABOUT.

WHAT'S MY PROBLEM ANYWAY? I MUST HAVE PMS, AS IN PREMENTAL SYNDROME OR SOMETHING. MAYBE I JUST MISS ANGEL SO MUCH THAT I'M HAVING A BREAKDOWN. MAYBE I CAN'T SURVIVE ON MY OWN, SO I HAVE TO GO AFTER OTHER PEOPLE'S BOYFRIENDS. OR MAYBE I'M JUST A HORRIBLE PERSON WHO DOESN'T DESERVE GOOD FRIENDS LIKE LIZ AND CONNER. UGH. LIZANDCONNER. WHY DOES THE SOUND OF THAT SUDDENLY BOTHER ME?

DID I SAY WAIT A DAY? MAYBE I SHOULD WAIT A WEEK.

CHAPTER 2

BAD, BIZARRE, AND WRONG

"I'm really sorry," Tia practiced as she rang the doorbell at the Wakefields' house on Sunday morning. Her self-imposed, twenty-four-hour grace period was over, and it was time to face the music. "I'm really, *really* sorry?" she tried, biting her lip nervously and attempting to find a good place for her hands. Putting them in the front pockets of her jeans was too casual, but hanging at her sides they felt totally awkward.

The problem was, there was no way *sorry* was going to be enough, and Tia, in all her jittery tension, knew it. But what was she supposed to say?

"I know how it looked, but it's not what you think?" Tia singsonged. It just sounded lame. She was about to turn around and retreat when Jessica finally opened the door. Tia's heart leaped into her throat.

"Hi, Jess," she said, immediately aware that her tone was too perky. Tia knew that after what had happened, there would already be a wall between her and Jessica. From the sour look on Jessica's face it was a big, fat, cinder-block wall.

Jessica shifted her weight and put one hand on her hip, staring at Tia with attitude to spare.

Tia squirmed in her canvas sneakers. "Uh . . . is Liz here?" she finally managed, wringing her hands so roughly, her fingertips were turning red.

Jessica snorted. "If you came to twist the knife, you're too late. Conner already beat you to it," she said, without shifting her gaze.

Tia felt like she had just shrunk four feet. "Jess, I feel so bad about this whole thing. You've got to believe me," Tia sputtered. "I never meant for this to happen—not that anything happened," she added quickly, holding up both palms. "Nothing did. Really. It was totally innocent. I mean, I know how it must have looked to Liz—" Tia closed her eyes and shook her head. "I don't even want to imagine what she thinks of me right now, but I can explain. In fact, I *need* to explain, so if you can just tell Liz that I'm here—"

"Oh, right," Jessica jeered, still grasping the doorknob. "Look, I seriously doubt Liz wants to talk to you right now. If I were you—" Jessica suddenly stopped and turned her head, and Tia could hear someone descending the stairs just inside the foyer. She stood on her toes to see over Jessica's shoulder and spotted Elizabeth on the landing.

"It's okay, Jess," Elizabeth said, sounding totally lifeless. Even from a distance Tia could see that her friend's eyes were red and puffy.

Jessica reluctantly opened the door, staring Tia down as she stepped over the threshold. Tia knew that look, and it made her stomach turn. It was the look Trent had given her when he'd found out that she had a boyfriend. It was the look Angel had given her when he'd found out she kissed Trent. What was happening to her? When had she turned into such a loser?

"I'll talk to you when I get home from work," Jessica called to her sister. Then she walked to the driveway and hopped in the Jeep. Tia watched until Jessica was out of sight, then closed the front door, feeling like an intruder in the normally welcoming home.

"Let's go into the living room," Elizabeth said, watching Tia almost indifferently. At least it was a step up from Jessica's death glare. She followed Elizabeth silently to the living room and sat down opposite her—Elizabeth on the sofa, Tia on the love seat.

Tia cleared her throat, deciding to jump right in. "Okay, first of all, I want to make sure that you know that absolutely nothing happened." She waited for some kind of relief to cross Elizabeth's features, but instead the girl's eyes flashed.

"Nice, Tia," she scoffed. "Why don't you try the truth?"

"What?" Tia blurted out. She couldn't help it. There wasn't a coherent thought in her head.

"Conner already told me you guys kissed," Elizabeth informed her, crossing her arms.

"He—" Tia snapped her mouth shut before she could say something stupid. But her mind was reeling. He'd told her. How could he do that? No possible good could come of it. And for some reason, her heart felt like it had just been pierced with an arrow. If he'd told Elizabeth, that meant it wasn't worth keeping a secret to him, which meant it meant nothing.

Nothing at all.

Which it should, Tia told herself. *Try to focus here.*

"What?" Elizabeth said, eyeing Tia with disdain. "You think we'd be better off if we all started *lying* to each other too?"

"N-No," Tia stammered. "I just . . . I didn't even think it was worth mentioning," she managed. "I mean, it was nothing. It was an accident, really. We were both half asleep, and he probably thought he was kissing you, you know?" She laughed nervously, wiping her sweaty palms against the sides of her jeans. "It's actually kind of funny when you think about it because I was probably dreaming about Angel, and he . . ."

Tia shut herself up when she saw Elizabeth's narrowed eyes and reddening skin.

"Funny?" Elizabeth asked, leaning forward in her seat. "I'm so glad you find this whole thing so amusing."

"No!" Tia responded, her heart racing. "Not

funny ha, ha—just funny *weird*, you know? Because neither one of us knew what we were doing, sort of like we were sleep walking or, well, sleep *kissing* or something."

Okay. This is not going well, Tia told herself as Elizabeth sat back stiffly, her eyes going blank. Tia laced her fingers together and started to fidget with her thumbs.

Well, at least she knew that Conner didn't want her. That was one less thing to worry about, right? She forced herself to breathe deeply. Right?

Elizabeth looked up at the ceiling and sighed. At least one of them seemed to be getting control of herself.

"I know what you're trying to say," Elizabeth said slowly.

"You do?" Tia really wished Elizabeth would clue her in.

"Yeah. Conner said the same thing—that it didn't mean anything to him," Elizabeth said, meeting Tia's eyes. Tia had to concentrate to keep from flinching at Elizabeth's words. "But I guess I'm just not sure how much that matters."

"What do you mean?" Tia asked.

"I mean—" Elizabeth gripped the edge of the couch cushion. "Why was Conner at your house all night anyway?"

"He just fell asleep with me—I mean, there. In my bed. Room. My bedroom." The words spilled from Tia's mouth faster than she could think.

Elizabeth's face was turning pink again. "But why was he there in the first place?"

"I guess because he was so freaked out about his mom coming home," Tia answered. "He just needed a place to veg."

"Exactly," Elizabeth said. Tia felt like some kind of net was slowly closing around her. "He needed someone to comfort him, and where did he go? Not to me, his girlfriend. He went to *you*."

That's true, he did, Tia thought, disgusted to realize that Elizabeth's words had made her feel oddly hopeful. *I'm a bad person,* she told herself. *Bad, bizarre, and wrong.* Tia rubbed her temples with her hands. She was here to make things better—not worse.

"But Conner and I have been friends for a long time. We've always talked about this stuff." Tia paused to make sure her mouth and her mind were in sync this time. "And he did try to go to you first, but you've been working so much lately that he just kept missing you." Tia tilted her head down, trying to catch Elizabeth's gaze. "Really, Liz. You're the one he wanted. You're the one he still wants." She watched Elizabeth closely, hoping for some sign that her words had made a difference, but Elizabeth just shrugged. At least she wasn't arguing.

"So," Tia said, waiting for Elizabeth to look up at her. "Friends?" she asked tentatively. She wrung her hands inside the front pouch of the Stanford sweatshirt she had bought way back when Angel had first been accepted there.

Elizabeth sighed—a sigh that seemed to last at least five minutes. Her gaze seemed to be permanently glued to the floor. "I don't know," she said finally, causing Tia's stomach to flop. "Right now I just want to be alone."

"Oh. Okay." Tia stood on shaky legs. She waited a moment, half expecting Elizabeth to get up and walk her to the door, but Elizabeth didn't move. Tia took a deep breath and headed for the foyer.

"I'll let myself out," she said quietly. There was nothing else left for her to do.

"I knew I should have stayed in bed today," Conner muttered, taking his place at the back of the line at House of Java. A woman walked past him with a steaming cup of cappuccino and a bagel on a plate, but when the line moved forward, Conner didn't budge.

"Hey, I know it's tough to get motivated on a Sunday morning," Andy said, clapping his friend on the back, "but look! Coffee. Straight ahead."

Conner nodded. It wasn't the coffee that was giving him pause. It was the person pouring the coffee. None other than Jessica Wakefield. He watched as an elderly man in a hat paid for his tea and moved along, but Conner stayed right where he was—five feet away from the counter.

"You snooze, you lose," Andy said, scooting past

him to the open register. "Hey, Jess, how's it going?" Andy asked in his annoyingly awake voice. Jessica peered past Andy with a scowl.

Good to see you too, Conner thought.

Andy glanced over his shoulder at Conner, obviously wondering what was up. Conner just shrugged. "Everything okay?" Andy asked Jessica.

"Fine," Jessica answered, her face softening once her attention was focused on Andy. "What can I get you?" she asked.

"I don't know," Andy said, rubbing his hands together and looking up at the board that listed the brews of the day. "I'm thinking I want to try something different."

"Really?" Jessica asked, raising her eyebrows and glaring at Conner again. "Gee, I thought Conner was the one who always had to have something new. He seems to get so easily bored with the same old thing, day in, day out."

Jessica was trying very hard to stare him down, but Conner just stared right back. Her immature antics didn't impress him. Besides, he had nothing to explain to Jessica. The only person he cared about was Elizabeth. And she was being too annoyingly stubborn to even talk to him.

Andy looked from Conner to Jessica and back again. "Am I missing something here?" he asked, but Conner just rolled his eyes and shook his head. "Okay," Andy said, leaning on the counter. "You know what? Forget what I said. I'll just have a small coffee with cream and sugar."

"No problem," Jessica said with a smile. She quickly grabbed a mug, added a spoonful of sugar and a squirt of cream, and then topped it off with hot coffee. "Is that it?" she asked, punching numbers into the cash register.

"Yeah, and whatever Conner's having," Andy answered. He flashed a twenty. "I'm paying."

No argument here, Conner thought, stepping up to the register. "I'll have a large coffee, black," he said. Jessica grabbed a mug and filled it with black liquid, slamming it down on the counter so hard, coffee sloshed over the sides.

"Sorry," she said, the corners of her mouth curved into a contemptuous smile. "That's three seventy-five," she said to Andy, her voice suddenly filled with genuine kindness again.

Andy handed her the twenty. "I'd tell you to keep the change, but then you'd just have to buy me lunch all week," he joked.

Jessica chuckled and handed him his change. "Thanks, *Andy,*" she said, ignoring Conner altogether. Then she turned her back on them and went about straightening up behind the counter.

Well, that was fun, Conner thought as he picked up his coffee and followed Andy to a table in the back. As soon as they had sat down, Andy leaned forward, his eyes wide.

"All right, explain something to me," Andy said. "If you're dating Wakefield sister A, what's up with all the tension between you and Wakefield sister B?"

"It's nothing, man," Conner grumbled. "Just drop it." He took a long sip of coffee, hoping that would be the end of the conversation, but Andy was still studying him.

"Look, if you don't tell me now, I'm just going to hear it all from Tia later," Andy said, shaking a packet of Sweet'n Low to add to the sugar already in his mug. At the mention of Tia's name, Conner almost spit the coffee out of his mouth. Instead he swallowed hard and nearly choked himself.

"Do me a favor," he said between coughs. "Don't mention this to Tee."

Andy rested one hand heavily on the table, his sweet tooth totally forgotten as he gave Conner his best reproachful look. "Oh, man," he said. "Tia is going to be pissed at you. You screwed things up with Elizabeth, didn't you?"

Conner took a sip of his coffee and looked away.

"That's too bad," Andy said. "I really thought you and Liz—" Conner glared at Andy and exhaled sharply. "Well, you know," Andy finished, looking into his coffee cup. They sat silently, the clinking of mugs around them filling the space in the conversation.

"So what happened?" Andy asked finally. Conner took another long sip of coffee and stared across the room at the door. "Not another girl, I hope."

Conner was used to being watched, but this time Andy's inquisitive stare made him antsy. He blinked twice—a gesture that wouldn't have meant anything to another person—but it was enough for Andy.

"Oh, *man*," Andy said, slumping back in his seat. He finally ripped open the Sweet'n Low and added it to his coffee, then took a long slug. Everything about him said *disappointment*.

"You're only half right," Conner said finally, feeling the sudden, inexplicable need to make Andy understand. If Andy told him everything was going to be fine, maybe he could get rid of the black cloud that had been hovering over him ever since yesterday morning.

"Half right?" he asked, holding his coffee in both hands as if he were warming them up. "Okay. What is this, one of Ms. Dixon's math quizzes?"

Conner smirked.

"So is there another girl or not?" Andy asked.

How was he supposed to answer that one? Conner leaned forward, resting his forearms on the table, knowing that if anyone other than Andy Marsden were sitting across from him, he wouldn't even bother. Period.

"Not really." He started to sip his coffee, then put it down. "Liz just *thinks* there is."

Andy sat up slightly. "And you haven't straightened her out," he said slowly.

"She won't talk to me," Conner said, staring into

the little black circle of liquid in his mug. He almost winced when Andy scooted forward in his seat, as if this was the most interesting news ever.

"Wait a second," Andy said. "That doesn't sound like Liz. Isn't she, like, the most levelheaded person on the planet? Why would she think there's someone else when there isn't and then not even talk to you about it?"

Conner looked down at his hands and sighed. He should never have let this conversation get this far.

"All right. What are you not telling me?"

That I'm a total screwup. Did I forget that part? Conner thought bitterly. He glanced at Andy's probing eyes. He could either tell the guy or let him hear it second- or thirdhand from someone who wouldn't even get the story right.

"Okay, so Liz saw me in bed with this other girl, and she totally freaked."

Andy's jaw dropped. "In *bed?*" he blurted out.

At that moment a cash register drawer slammed closed with tremendous force. Conner looked up just in time to see Jessica glaring at him from behind the counter. He waved to her with equal contempt, and Jessica stalked off to the back room.

When Conner turned his attention back to Andy, the kid was as pale as a ghost and obviously at a loss for words. Unfortunately Conner knew that wouldn't last.

"You were—you know—and Liz saw you?" Andy stammered.

"We weren't *you know*," Conner said, gripping the sides of the table as he leaned forward. "And Liz didn't see anything. She just thinks she did."

Andy narrowed his eyes. "Okay, explain this to me. You were in bed with another girl, but you were just, what, having a slumber party?"

Conner scowled. "I fell asleep there," he said. "Is that so hard to believe?"

"No, not at all," Andy said sarcastically. "Random girls invite me over to spend the night all the time."

"It wasn't some random girl," Conner said, his jaw clenching and unclenching. "It was Tia."

"*What!*"

"Shhh!" Conner hissed, leaning so far forward, his butt came off his seat.

Andy collapsed back into his chair, looking like a deflated pool toy. "I think my life is passing before my eyes," he said quietly.

Can you say "melodrama"? Conner thought.

"Look. I went over there to hang out Friday night. We watched a movie and fell asleep, and then Liz walked in the next morning and flipped out." Andy was still staring. "Nothing happened," Conner said slowly. He propped his feet up on the chair next to his. "I mean, we may have kissed once," he added as casually as possible, "but I don't even remember. It was nothing."

Andy didn't move a muscle, but his eyes finally focused, and he looked up at Conner. "Do you realize

38

what you've done?" he said slowly, in a tone that made Conner's insides squirm. "You've changed everything," he said. "Everything."

With a huge sigh Conner leaned back in his seat and brought his hands to his face, tilting back his head. Why did Andy have this talent for saying exactly what Conner didn't want to hear?

"Two caffè lattes and a slice of chocolate-raspberry cheesecake," Jessica said, sliding two mugs and a plate down the counter to Jeremy.

"Thanks," Jeremy said, flashing her a quick smile. "That's . . . seven-fifty," he told the couple at the register as he rang it all up.

"Here you go," said the woman, passing Jeremy a ten. "And put the change in your tip cup. You two make a great team." She smiled conspiratorially at Jessica, who blushed beet red. The woman obviously thought they were a couple or something.

Why would she think that? It wasn't like Jeremy and Jessica were still emitting couple vibes after all this time. Hopefully.

Jessica watched Jeremy add the two dollars and fifty cents to the money in the large, glass tip cup on top of the register. Then he pulled it all out and started counting out of the view of the customers. He looked so satisfied with himself as a smug little smile crept across his face. Jessica felt a strange flutter in her stomach. Was it her, or had he suddenly gotten even cuter?

"Hey, partner," Jeremy said, looking over at her with his deep brown eyes. "She wasn't kidding. We're up to almost twenty dollars in here. That's the most I've ever seen in the tip cup."

"Twenty—really?" Jessica asked. "We must be doing *something* right." She cocked her head and brought one finger to her chin. "Hmmm . . . maybe you actually made some drinkable coffee this time," she teased.

"Possibly," Jeremy said, not missing a beat. "But it probably has more to do with the fact that you finally figured out the ever confusing difference between regular and decaf."

Jessica smirked. "It could be that." She nodded and straightened the straws in the dispenser. "Or maybe the women have been tipping big to thank you for *not* hitting on them," she suggested with a straight face.

"Actually," Jeremy said, "I think it's your managerial style. I'm sure everyone can just sense how brilliant and in control you are." He patted her on the back as he walked to the sink for a dishcloth.

Jessica's heart thumped. Was that a dig? Had Jeremy Aames just mocked her to her face? When Jeremy turned around again, he was smiling. And there wasn't a trace of malice behind it. Jessica almost rolled her eyes at herself. How could there be? Jeremy didn't know the meaning of the word *malice*.

"You know, you're probably right," she mused,

getting back into playful mode. "In fact, I should probably just keep the whole twenty myself."

"Just try it," Jeremy said, quickly flexing his muscles. Jessica laughed and looked around the café as he began wiping the counters. It was a little after one, and the crowd was thinning out. Things wouldn't pick up again until three-thirty or so, when the matinee let out across the street.

"Hey, Jeremy," she said. "I'm going to bus a few tables while it's slow—are you all set back here?"

Jeremy snapped to attention on the spot. "Ma'am, yes, ma'am," he responded in true military style.

There it was again. The subtle dig. Maybe. Jessica wasn't sure if she could handle always trying to guess what he was thinking, so she decided to take a cue from Ally.

"Jeremy, are you mad at me because I got promoted?"

Jeremy fell out of the rigid military pose and scrunched up his forehead.

"Are you kidding?" Jeremy asked. "Don't worry about it."

The tone was sincere, but he went right back to counter wiping, avoiding eye contact at all costs. There was definitely something different between them today, if she could only figure out what.

"Are you sure?" she pressed, leaning on the counter so he'd have to stop working. "I mean, maybe you should talk to Ally about it. She must have had some reason for—"

Jeremy tucked his chin and chuckled. "Look, Jessica, it's okay, really. I was a little . . . annoyed at first, but I talked to Ally, and it's all good." He caught her eye and smiled. "Besides, if I have to take orders from someone, I'm glad it's you."

The blush came back full force, and Jessica looked away. "Thanks."

"No problem," he said. "So stop worrying about it and give me my orders, Sergeant," he added with a mock salute.

Jessica rolled her eyes. "You're such a jerk," she said, smirking. She grabbed the deep plastic tray and sponge used for clearing tables and started to walk past him. "Oh, wait," she said, stopping suddenly and setting her things on the counter. "I should probably cash out this machine before the next shift starts." She grabbed the key from around her wrist and put it in the cash register, then pushed a few buttons, but nothing happened. "Hello?" she said, repeating the process.

"You okay over there?" Jeremy asked, glancing over his shoulder.

"Am I doing something wrong?" Jessica asked, jabbing at the buttons. She pressed the total button and turned her key one more time, but once again nothing happened.

She tapped the side of the cash register with her

hand, trying to figure out if she'd forgotten a step. But before she could even mentally run through the procedure, she heard Jeremy chuckle behind her and narrowed her eyes. She was just about to turn and bawl him out when she felt his hands on her shoulders. Which made her heart skip. She wondered if that would ever fully go away.

"Wait, let me show you," he said, gently moving her aside. "You just have to jiggle it like this . . . and then . . ." Jessica watched as Jeremy turned the key back and forth twice and then pressed a few buttons, sending the cash drawer flying out.

"Hey!" she said, leaning over the register as if she were scolding it. "That's exactly what I did! Why did it work for you?"

Jeremy brushed at the front of his apron cockily. "Because I'm the man."

"Very funny," Jessica scoffed, hip chucking him lightly.

"It's no big deal, actually," Jeremy said, lifting one shoulder. "The key just sticks a little, so you have to wiggle it really quick until you feel it click in."

"Oh." Jessica scowled. "How did you know that?"

"Daniel usually has me cash out when he's managing, and I've watched Ally do it a million times," Jeremy explained.

Jessica stared after him as he went back to work. She was really beginning to wonder why Ally had promoted her and not him. He obviously knew ten times more about running the place than she did.

She grabbed the balancing sheet from under the cash drawer and started totaling up the money. The bills made a crisp flapping sound as she counted them from one hand to the other, and Jessica was surprised by how much fun it was to feel so in charge. She felt a smile forming on her face as she added everything together, balancing to the penny.

Okay. I can do this, she thought, writing down the new total and replacing all of the money in the drawer. She started to close it, but Jeremy stopped her.

"Um, you're not going to leave all that cash in there, are you?" he asked.

Jessica froze uncertainly. "Well, yeah . . . why?" she asked, looking at the drawer as if it could answer her.

"It's just, well . . . don't you think you should maybe take out some of the big bills and put them in the safe?" he asked.

Jessica squeezed her eyes shut. "I knew I was forgetting something." She let the drawer slide out again, removing a fifty and several twenties.

Stupid, she thought, realizing she was coming off as totally clueless. "Thanks," she muttered quickly.

"No problem," Jeremy said, running his dishcloth under a stream of steaming water. "You might want to take a few tens too so you can get quarters and ones from the safe."

Jessica exhaled sharply and leaned into the counter with a thud. "Jeremy," she said tersely, waiting for him to turn around. "Can I ask you something?"

Jeremy drew back a little, obviously surprised by her tone. "Shoot."

"When you talked to Ally, what reason did she give you? For promoting me instead of you, I mean. It's not like I'm more qualified or anything," she said, waving a frustrated hand toward the cash register.

Jeremy leaned back against the counter and crossed one ankle over the other. "You really want to know?"

Jessica nodded.

"Well, Ally said it was time for me to get a life outside of work," he said with a self-deprecating grin.

For a second Jessica just stood there. So, basically, she *was* the second choice for the job. She tried not to let this tidbit of information irritate her and went for the lighthearted response. "Ouch. Harsh," she said, grimacing.

"Yeah, well, you know Ally." Jeremy chuckled. "She doesn't exactly beat around the bush."

"So . . . what do you think about that?" Jessica asked. Just then she heard the bell above the door clang, and she looked over to see Jade walking toward them, wearing a pair of beat-up overalls and a T-shirt and still managing to look like she'd just stepped out of the pages of a fashion magazine. Like she always did.

"I think she's right," Jeremy said in a low voice.

Jessica turned back to him. "What do you—," she started, but it was obvious that their conversation was over. Jeremy wasn't even looking at her anymore. His eyes were trained on Jade. Trained on Jade like she'd just walked in sporting a bikini and a smile. Jessica tried to ignore the sinking feeling in the pit of her stomach.

"Hey, Jade," Jeremy said with a smile.

"Jeremy," Jade returned.

There was something about the way they had said each other's names that made Jessica's shoulders tighten.

"Hi, Jade," she said, her voice cracking as she smiled weakly. "Is this your first official shift?"

"I guess so." Jade flashed a wide grin. "I trained with Daniel a little yesterday, but only for like an hour. But don't worry. I can assure you I'm eminently qualified for the position," she said, holding up her index finger. "I've already had five cups of coffee this morning." She nodded at Jeremy. "I just hope you're ready because I'm fully caffeinated and good to go."

With that, Jade strode to the back room, Jeremy's eyes following her every move.

Jessica watched him uneasily, aware that the tightness in her shoulders had spread to her neck. She tilted her head first to one side, then to the other, trying to loosen up a little.

What was wrong with her? If anything, she

should be happy that she and Jeremy had cleared up the whole promotion/tension thing. But she was somehow feeling anything but happy. Jessica rubbed her temples and glanced at Jeremy, who looked like he'd entered the daydream plane.

Suddenly she was beginning to wish that Jade had stayed with the drunks at First and Ten.

Andy Marsden

Reasons why I'm glad I didn't consult Conner about my . . . sexuality issues, even though I wasn't exactly <u>planning</u> on it when I invited him to HOJ:

1. He's not exactly Mr. Sensitivity.

2. He might think I was coming on to him since it seems like everyone else is these days. (Note to self: Find Tia and see if her pupils look dilated or if she's speaking in tongues.)

3. Looking at the way he runs his own life, I bet his advice would probably be to avoid thinking at all costs.

4. It's quite possible that the boy just might have even more issues than me.

The Next Big Rumor

"Ramirez," called Ms. Dalton without looking up from her attendance sheet.

"Here," Tia grumbled. *Unfortunately.* The tiny hairs on the back of her neck kept standing up and sending shivers down her spine.

Jessica must be giving me another death stare, she thought, sinking farther down in her seat. She glanced over one row and up two seats and saw Conner's profile. He was leaning forward on his desk, his gaze rigidly fixed toward the front of the room, like an overzealous honor student not wanting to miss one word of the teacher's lecture. Problem was, this was homeroom.

Tia eyed his dark sunglasses and the way his jaw was set forward, his arms folded defiantly. Okay, so he was an overzealous honor student with a lot of attitude.

Conner sat silently, clenching and unclenching his jaw. Tia watched as the tiny muscles at the base of his cheek kept popping out. She felt awful for him. It was bad enough that he had to deal with his

49

mother coming back from rehab, but now he had to add a love triangle into the mix too.

No. Not a love triangle. Just a mix-up. Conner would have to be attracted to her to make this a love triangle, and he obviously wasn't.

She watched as Conner raised one arm to his forehead, supporting it. His back rose and fell with each slow breath, and she wished there was something she could do for him. But she couldn't even talk to him without making Jessica think there was something going on. And Jessica would definitely report back to Elizabeth, which would only create even more drama. If that was even possible.

If only I hadn't let him stay, Tia thought. She stared at the clock, willing the arms to move backward until it was Friday night again so she could do it over and get it right the second time around. If she had just gone to the Riot like she was supposed to and made Conner go talk to Elizabeth, none of this ever would have happened.

"Wakefield," called Ms. Dalton, snapping Tia back to attention.

"Here," Jessica's voice resounded, two rows back. The boldness of it made Tia squirm. She sounded so confident and . . . threatening. Tia glanced at the clock again, noting that the minute hand seemed to be moving extra slow this morning. Tia let her head fall onto the desk, her forehead pressing into the cold, faux-wood laminate.

"Is something wrong, Tia?" an overly concerned voice asked from two desks over.

Oh, come on, Tia thought. *This has to be a bad dream.* She turned slightly, just enough to see Melissa Fox perched on her desktop like a hawk.

Melissa was sitting with her back toward the front of the room and her feet on the seat of her chair so that she could talk to Will, who occupied the desk behind her. Tia almost groaned. With Jessica glaring at her from behind and Conner ignoring her from the front, she wasn't sure she could deal with the couple from hell at her side.

Wearily she looked at Melissa, whose twinkling eyes were the same pale blue as Will's oxford. Tia had never met anyone else who thrived on other people's misery the way Melissa did. Melissa smirked and glanced toward the front of the room at Conner. Tia drew back.

"Trouble in paradise?" Melissa asked with a self-satisfied grin.

Tia's heart froze. If Melissa thought there was something juicy going on, she'd dig until she figured out what it was. And the last thing Tia needed was for any of this to get around school.

She straightened herself up and cleared her throat. "Ms. Dalton?" she called, waiting for her teacher to look up from the attendance report she was busily filling out.

"Yes?"

"Is it safe for Melissa to be sitting on her desk that way?" Tia asked, her eyes wide and innocent.

Ms. Dalton glanced toward Melissa and Will. "No. Melissa, could you face forward, please?" she said, going back to her report. Melissa narrowed her eyes at Tia, then reluctantly turned and sat down in her seat.

Tia came very close to cracking a smile. Then she felt the hairs on her neck stand up again. Was the minute hand on the clock *ever* going to move?

"Okay," Maria said as Jessica set her lunch tray down across from Ken's. "Spill."

Great. Another round of what's-up-with-Liz-and-Conner? Jessica thought. All morning she had been saying "it's no big deal" and "everything's fine" while gossipmonger after dirt digger had come to her to get the scoop. Even Todd Wilkins had made a point of asking if Elizabeth was okay.

"Spill what?" Jessica asked, taking a bite of a chicken nugget. She looked at Ken blankly, and he just shrugged. Maybe if they were both totally disinterested, Maria would drop it.

No such luck.

"Are you kidding? Spill *what?*" Maria mimicked, dropping her turkey burger. "Liz and Conner. Has it escaped your attention that they're not talking to each other?"

"Maybe you should ask Liz," Jessica said, sighing

heavily and sitting back in her hard plastic chair. "I really don't want to talk about it without her around." She pushed another nugget into her barbecue sauce, trying not to look too pleased with her response. She was certain the noble-sister approach would strike a chord with Maria.

"I already did," Maria responded, stealing a french fry from Ken's plate and popping it into her mouth. "But all Liz would say was that I should feel lucky I was spared a relationship with Conner."

"No, *I* should feel lucky," Ken said, taking a cookie from Maria's tray. The girl blushed, and all Jessica wanted to do was barf from the sweetness of it all.

"So what did the jerk do anyway?" Maria asked, refusing to drop the subject. She glanced around the cafeteria. "And where's Tia? She must have the dirtiest of the dirt."

You have no idea, Jessica thought. She closed her eyes and took a deep breath, letting it out slowly.

"Oh my God!" Maria said suddenly. "Did Tia do something too?"

Jessica scowled. "Why would you think that?" she asked, looking at Ken for help. Ken ate a french fry.

"Your face," Maria said, pointing at Jessica and looking triumphant. "Tia and Conner both did something." But a moment later her expression turned shocked and then completely fell. "But what could they really do together besides—" Maria

53

paused suddenly, glancing furtively at Ken.

Jessica squeezed her eyes shut and groaned. "I told you we shouldn't be talking about this," she said, the hiss of her whisper cutting the air.

Maria shook her head. "Oh, come on. You have to tell us now," she insisted.

Jessica looked from Maria to Ken and back again. "All right," she said, leaning forward so both of them could hear her hushed voice. "But this cannot leave this table." Maria and Ken nodded. "Saturday morning Liz went over to Tia's and walked in on Tia and Conner in bed together."

"What!" Maria screeched. Jessica was about to tell her to shut up when she heard an explosion of laughter from the table behind her. Her stomach immediately shrank to the size of a pea. Jessica would know that laughter anywhere.

It had been directed at her for weeks.

She watched as Ken and Maria's eyes widened and Maria squirmed a bit in her seat. Jessica leaned forward so far on the table, her hair fell into her food.

"Please, please, *please* don't tell me Melissa and her friends are sitting right behind me," she whispered so quietly, she could barely even hear herself.

Ken leaned in close. "Melissa and her friends are sitting right behind you."

Jessica's heart stopped for way too long, and she squeezed her eyes shut again. How could she have possibly opened her mouth without checking the immediate vicinity? Had she learned nothing in her three-plus years at high school?

"They didn't hear you," Maria said hopefully. "How could they?"

"Yeah, right," Jessica muttered, pushing away her tray. She refused to give Melissa the satisfaction of checking over her shoulder, but she knew if she did, she'd see the telltale Fox smirk.

Jessica Wakefield had just started the next big rumor at Sweet Valley High.

"Can anyone tell me why Rossetti's poem about honeybees is so poignant?" Mr. Quigley asked. Conner looked around the silent classroom. Two girls in the corner were studying their textbooks intently, as if the answer was about to jump out and smack them on the nose. Andy, who usually answered all of Quigley's questions—at least with a joke—was doodling in his notebook, more distracted than usual. And Elizabeth . . .

Wake up, Liz, Conner willed her. *You live for this stuff.* But she continued to sit still, slumped in her chair like a rag doll.

He cleared his throat. "Because bee stings hurt?" he ventured, receiving only a scowl from Mr. Quigley and a few giggles from the girls in the corner. He stared at Elizabeth.

Come on! That's the lamest thing I've ever said in

my life, he silently told her. How could she possibly let it go without even a contemptuous glare? But there was nothing. Elizabeth hadn't given him an inch all day. Not when he beaned her on the shoulder with little bits of rolled-up paper and not even when he had volunteered to read some stupid poem about goblins.

Luckily the bell rang before anyone else had a chance to venture a guess at Quigley's question.

"Be sure to read the rest of the Rossetti poems for tomorrow's class, and keep working on your pieces for Friday," Mr. Quigley called as the students began to file out of the room. All Conner could focus on was Elizabeth's back disappearing out the door.

He rose quickly and ran after her, finally catching her in the hall. "Liz, wait," he called, placing his hand on her shoulder. "We need to talk." He felt Elizabeth tense at his touch, and he let his hand drop away. Reluctantly she turned to face him. It was the first time Conner had gotten a good look at her all day, and he suddenly realized that she wasn't wearing any makeup.

She was so fragile. And so perfect. He raised his hand, touching it lightly to her cheek. Elizabeth flinched, and Conner felt it in his chest.

"Look," he started, "nothing happened with Tia." Elizabeth blinked and looked away, watching the students buzzing through the hall. Conner stepped to the side, blocking her view so that she had to look at him.

"I just need to be alone for a while," she said quietly.

"Come on, Liz, I know you," Conner said, leaning one shoulder against the lockers. "The more you think about it, the worse you're going to make it in your head."

Elizabeth sniffed, curving one side of her mouth slightly. "Maybe," she said softly. "But I still need some time."

Conner looked into her desolate blue-green eyes. Why couldn't she just believe him? Why did she have to psychoanalyze everything? He wanted to reach out and grab her, shake her, kiss her—do anything that would make her realize nothing had changed. He was still the same person he had been three days ago. But before he knew it, she was walking away.

"Liz," he murmured, but she kept walking. Conner felt the heat of his frustration boiling up within his body and gathering in his clenched fists. He contemplated striking out at the shiny gray lockers, but he was aware that people were already staring at him as they walked by.

Move along. Nothing to see here, he thought, glaring at an overinterested freshman girl. *Nothing at all.*

Ken Matthews

I just realized girls are right about guys. Here's my evidence:

My dad is cheating on Asha.

Conner is cheating on Liz, and he already cheated on Maria.

Will Simmons cheated on Melissa with Jessica and then cheated on Jessica with Melissa.

Josh Radinsky is keeping a list in the back of his math notebook of which girls he's hooked up with, and he's shown it to just about everyone he knows.

And I'm not even surprised by any of this stuff anymore.

So girls are right. Guys are jerks.

CHAPTER

Breaking the Rules

4

"And don't forget to tell people about the free gift pack with every purchase over twenty-five dollars," said Carolee, the manager at Sedona, as Elizabeth began her afternoon shift. Carolee examined her reflection in the large mirror behind the counter, fluffing out her sandy blond mane and making sure that her eyelashes weren't clumping. When she was done, she smiled at herself and turned to Elizabeth, scanning her face as if she was performing a mental makeover.

"Elizabeth," she said, articulating each syllable in a way that accentuated her boldly outlined lips. "Why don't you take advantage of some of the samples?" She swept her manicured hand over the multicolored bottles and compacts at one of the makeover stations. "It's always a good idea to freshen your face while it's slow. Maybe you could get rid of those bags under your eyes. You look like you haven't slept in days, and in this business you need to look your best if you want to cash in on the commissions." She rubbed her thumb against her fingers as if she were rubbing a bunch of dollar bills together.

"Okay," Elizabeth managed, nodding weakly.

"Excellent," Carolee said with a smile. Then she patted Elizabeth on the shoulder and gave her a double thumbs-up before shuffling around to the other side of the counter, her three-inch heels clicking all the way. Elizabeth sighed. Carolee had a tendency to go overboard in her little debriefing sessions. It was as if she thought they were working at a nuclear testing facility instead of a makeup counter. One bad application of eyeliner and the whole place was going to blow.

Then again, Carolee did have a lot more experience peddling cosmetics than Elizabeth, and it was clear she hadn't intended for her pep talk to come off as criticism. Giving makeup advice was probably as close as Carolee had ever come to showing some kind of maternal concern.

Elizabeth ran her hand over the numerous colors on the shade palette in front of her. She grabbed a brush and dabbed at the dark circles with concealer, but it didn't make a difference, and it just made her sore eyes sting even more.

"This sucks," Elizabeth muttered, tossing the brush back onto the counter.

"Excuse me? Aren't you supposed to be convincing people to buy this stuff?"

The familiar voice jolted Elizabeth at first, but

then she looked up and forced a smile. "Hi, Mom," she said brightly. "What are you doing here?" As if she didn't know. Her mother's eyes were full of *real* maternal concern. The kind Carolee couldn't pull off if she tried.

Mrs. Wakefield shrugged. "My meeting with the Wilsons went faster than I expected, and I wound up with some free time this afternoon. So I thought, why not go to Sedona for a makeover? After all, I've been meaning to come in ever since you started here. Got a minute?"

Elizabeth looked up and down the counter at the empty seats. "I think I can squeeze you in," she said wryly.

Mrs. Wakefield laughed and boosted herself up into one of the black-vinyl-and-chrome chairs. "Ooh," she exclaimed, rubbing a hand along her cheek as she looked into the large, oval mirror in front of her. "Can you turn that thing around? I don't think I need all of these wrinkles magnified."

Elizabeth let a puff of air escape through her nose—the nearest she'd come to laughing all day. "Sure," she said, flipping the mirror around to its normal-view side. "So what can I do for you today, ma'am?" she asked, trying to emphasize each syllable and push out her lips the way Carolee did.

Mrs. Wakefield shook her head back like a model in a hair commercial. "I need a new look," she said. "This middle-aged-mother thing is getting old."

Elizabeth cracked a smile. "Okay. So what are you going for? Fresh-faced, thirteen-year-old cover girl? Or maybe we should go to the other extreme and give you a goth look. . . ."

Mrs. Wakefield pretended to think it over. "Hmmm. *I* could do goth," she hedged, "but I'm afraid your father would be a bit put off by all the black eyeliner." Elizabeth shook her head and chuckled in spite of everything. "How about slightly hip, middle-aged mom?" Mrs. Wakefield suggested.

Elizabeth nodded and reached for a tub of cold cream. "I think we can do that," she said. She gently massaged a small amount of lotion onto her mother's face and then removed her old makeup with a soft flannel cloth. Then, when Mrs. Wakefield's face radiated clean, Elizabeth reached for a tube of foundation and began working it into her mother's skin.

"So," Mrs. Wakefield said slowly as Elizabeth squeezed some more of the rosy beige cream onto her hands. "How are you doing?" *Here it comes,* Elizabeth thought. *The interrogation.* "Okay," she answered slowly.

Mrs. Wakefield nodded. "Good," she said, leaning back a little and closing her eyes while Elizabeth worked on her forehead. *Is that it?* Elizabeth wondered, staring at her mother's bluish white eyelids. Was her mother actually going to let it go with "okay"?

"And how are things with you and Conner?" Mrs. Wakefield asked, her eyes still closed. "Any better?"

Elizabeth felt her shoulders relax. It was the opening she had been waiting for. "Not really," she said, dusting her mother's face with blush. "I mean, I'm not as hysterical as I was at home yesterday, but nothing's changed."

"Do you want to tell me what happened?" Mrs. Wakefield asked.

Yes, Elizabeth thought. *Yes, yes, yes.* She felt like a little girl with a scraped knee who had just been whisked into her mother's arms. But as much as she wanted to just spill all the details, the words didn't want to come. Part of her didn't want her mother to hate Conner, which she undoubtedly would once she heard the story.

She wanted her mother to forgive him as much as she wanted to be able to forgive him herself.

She finished shading her mother's right cheek and examined her face to make sure the blush was even on both sides. Then she put down the large brush and grabbed a smaller, foam-tipped one to apply the eye shadow. Streaking her mother's eyelids with a shade of light brown, Elizabeth cleared her throat and began to talk slowly.

"You know how I went to see Conner on Saturday morning?" she asked. Her mother nodded. "Well, he wasn't at home, and Megan said she didn't think he had been home all night." She waited for a gasp from her mother—a flinching movement, a slight shifting of position—anything to suggest that Mrs. Wakefield was passing judgment, but there was nothing. "I guess he and his mom have been fighting a lot since she came back," Elizabeth added.

"That must be tough on him," Mrs. Wakefield said.

"Yeah, I guess," Elizabeth responded, tilting her head slightly. She ran the eye wand through a pat of dark brown powder and brushed it across the crease in her mother's eyelid. "So anyway, I went over to Tia's to see if she knew where he was, and he was there. In her bedroom. He spent the night with her."

Mrs. Wakefield's eyes sprang open. Elizabeth braced herself for the onslaught of indignation. But it didn't come.

"I see," her mother said finally, relaxing back into the chair again. "Have you talked to him about it?"

Okay, this was a bit too freaky.

"A little," Elizabeth answered. "I mean, he's been trying to talk to me, but I haven't really been in the mood to listen."

"Well, it's important that you take your time and listen to yourself first," Mrs. Wakefield said, nodding. She paused a moment and cleared her throat. "Elizabeth?" she began. "Have *you* considered sleeping with Conner?"

"Mom!" Elizabeth exclaimed, almost dropping the makeup.

"I'm just asking," her mother said, raising her hands defensively.

Elizabeth stared at her, wide-eyed. "*God . . .* no," she said. "I mean, it's not like Tia and Conner were having sex. They were just . . . *sleeping*. And they both say nothing happened."

Except, of course, for the kiss, Elizabeth reminded herself, causing her stomach to turn.

"Do you believe them?" Mrs. Wakefield asked.

"I don't know," Elizabeth said, slowly setting the eye shadow on the glass countertop and sitting down across from her mother. "I guess I should, but—" Elizabeth stared at the ceiling and shook her head. "I don't know. I just feel . . . betrayed, I guess."

Mrs. Wakefield leaned forward and put her hand on top of Elizabeth's in her lap. "Maybe you should hear him out," she said, looking into Elizabeth's eyes. "You might stop feeling betrayed if you at least hear the truth."

Elizabeth could hardly believe what she was hearing. Her mother? Telling her to give Conner the Bad Boy a chance? It was like she'd stepped into an alternate universe.

"Ya think?" Elizabeth asked, raising her eyebrows.

Her mother cracked a grin. "All I know is, if I hadn't given your father a chance to explain some of the stuff he's done over the years, we never would have even made it to the altar, let alone through years of marriage and three kids!"

Elizabeth laughed and shook her head, enjoying the small release the laughter gave her. "Let's finish this makeover," she said, picking up the eye shadow again. "You need a hip young look to go with your new hip young attitude."

"Yeah, right," her mother said sarcastically, closing her eyes again. "My heart's still recovering from the idea of you having sex."

"I wouldn't worry about it," Elizabeth said, watching as a relieved little smile played about her mother's lips. There. That was the least she could do for her mom. Especially considering she was about as far from getting physical with Conner as possible.

She couldn't even imagine being close to him again because whenever she did, she remembered just how close he'd been with Tia.

"Go, Gladiators," Tia whispered to herself with mock enthusiasm. As she walked down the empty corridor, she lifted one of her pom-poms into the air and shook it halfheartedly, finally letting her arm drop to her side in a limp arc. She should actually be psyched. The day from hell was finally over. With the exception of French class—where she had to deal with Jessica, Melissa, Maria, *and* Elizabeth—cheerleading practice had been the worst part. Tia was certain that if she had spent one more minute with that goofy, fake smile plastered on her face, she definitely would have lost her lunch. Not that she had actually eaten any.

All through practice Tia had forced herself to act like nothing was wrong, like her life *wasn't* falling apart. It was partly out of loyalty to the squad. After all, she was the captain, and even if her personal life was being torn to bits, she couldn't let it affect the team. But Tia knew that she was keeping up the front partially because of Melissa Fox.

The whole time they were working out, she had felt Melissa staring at her with those steel blue eyes like she was waiting for something. It gave Tia the creeps. Once Melissa had even made a point of asking Tia about her weekend, commenting loudly that she didn't look like she had gotten a lot of sleep. But Tia had managed to keep it together, and to Jessica's credit, so had she.

Still, it was obvious that Melissa knew something, which was pretty scary. If Melissa got her hands on this story, there was no telling what she would do with it. The girl had major issues. Which was probably why she was such a vindictive, two-faced, manipulative little—

Tia's thought process came to an abrupt halt when she rounded the corner. There, leaning against her locker, was Conner, and her heart skipped at the sight of him. Which was definitely not good. And she'd thought the day from hell was over.

"Conner," she said, approaching him slowly, as if there might be a hidden camera somewhere in the hallway.

"Tee. I am so glad to see you," he said, pushing away from the locker. His tired but relieved face caught her by surprise, as did her overwhelming urge to hug him. But what was so bad about that? After all, he was still her friend. Her best friend. And hadn't they hugged or pecked each other on the cheek a million times before? So why should it be any different now?

"What are you doing here?" she asked, tilting her head to one side. The words sounded harsher than she had intended.

"Uh . . . waiting for you?" he suggested sarcastically, stuffing his hands into the front pockets of his jeans.

"That's not what I meant," Tia said, rolling her eyes.

Conner nodded and looked away. "I know," he said, stopping short of an apology. Tia glanced at his deep green eyes. She had been looking into those eyes for over ten years now, and she always had been able to read almost every expression Conner had. Until now. Something had changed, but what she couldn't figure out was if it was something in her, something in him, or something in both of them.

Tia twisted her pom-poms back and forth in her left hand, the rustle of them filling the quiet hall.

"You want to go for a drive?" Conner asked, finally breaking the stillness.

Tia's stomach flopped. This was getting ridiculous. This was Conner. There had to be some way to get control of these little physical reactions before she drove herself crazy.

"It's a yes-or-no question, Tee," he prompted.

"Um, I'd like to." She hesitated, focusing on his feet. *Finish the sentence,* she willed herself. "But I don't know. . . . I just think it would be better if we lay low for a while."

"*Lay low?*" Conner echoed in his standard obnoxious tone. "What the hell does that mean?"

Tia lifted her chin, feeling a tiny bit of defiance surge up in her chest. At least it was better than the bizarre mushy sensations she'd been having. When it came to Conner, the urge to put him in his place was familiar.

"It means I don't think we should hang out together until this mess gets straightened out," she said coolly, folding her arms over her chest.

Conner looked like he had about a million things he wanted to say at that moment, but Tia knew he wasn't one for verbosity.

"Fine. Whatever," he said, turning on his heel. "Call me when you grow up." He stalked off down the hall, not even pausing to look back.

Tia took a deep breath and let it out shakily, forcing herself to take control.

"You did the right thing," she told herself quietly, hoping that saying it aloud would make it true. "This will all blow over soon. You're fine." Unfortunately the tears in her eyes disproved her words.

"Jeremy!" Jade said, going from slumped over the counter to standing up straight in half a second. "I'm *so* glad you're here."

Not a bad reception.

"What's up?" Jeremy asked, shrugging off his jacket as he joined her behind the counter at HOJ. Every time he saw Jade, she seemed to get prettier. Today she was wearing a black V-necked T-shirt and a colorful beaded necklace. Her shiny hair was pulled back into two buns at the back of her head. She almost looked like a doll. Except for the disturbed, yet somehow amused, expression in her eyes.

"It's Ally," she said, swiftly grabbing a full coffeepot and pouring its contents into a metal carafe on the countertop. "She's totally freaking out."

As if on cue, Ally rushed out of the back room, pale as a sheet. "Jeremy! I need you to run an errand for me right away."

"What's wrong?" Jeremy asked. He hadn't seen Ally so crazed since their coffee supplier had discontinued decaf almond hazelnut.

"Milk," Ally said, throwing one hand up in the air. "We're out of milk. The delivery guy called, and his shipment has been delayed, so he won't be coming until tomorrow." Jeremy tried to look sympathetic, but it was hard to keep a straight face while

Jade stood behind Ally, twirling her index finger in circles next to her head and crossing her eyes.

"Okay. Calm down," Jeremy said. "We'll just—"

Ally reached out and firmly placed her hand on his shoulder, stopping him cold.

"I need you to run down to the supermarket and buy them out," Ally said, stuffing a wad of bills into his hand. "Skim, whole, half-and-half—whatever they have. We just need enough to get through the night. Understand?"

"Got it," Jeremy said, grabbing his jacket again. He was glad for an excuse to look away from Jade's antics before he lost it completely.

"And take Jade with you," Ally added, turning around quickly. Jeremy's heart dropped, but Jade was faster than Ally. By the time Ally was facing her, Jade's hands were neatly folded across her chest, and her face was the picture of innocence—eyes widened sympathetically, forehead creased with concern.

Jeremy couldn't help grinning. Jade was definitely going to be interesting to have around.

"I can cover things here," Ally assured them, pushing her brown hair back from her face. "Just be quick."

"Oh, we will," Jade said. Before Jeremy could even speak, she'd grabbed him by the hand and was leading him out the door. "You heard the woman," she said quietly. "We have to hurry."

Outside, Jade held on to Jeremy's hand and

started down the sidewalk. Jeremy blushed but didn't pull away. He kind of liked the feel of her fingers around his.

"Wait," Jeremy said, pulling back on her arm. "I'm parked out back."

"That's why we're taking my car," Jade said, guiding him to a faded, red, vintage Volkswagen Beetle. Jeremy stopped short when he noticed its beat-up exterior, but Jade wasn't fazed. "Isn't it cute?" she asked. "It was my mom's when she was in high school."

Jade finally released his hand and jogged to the driver's side, leaving Jeremy acutely aware of the cold spot in the center of his palm where her hand had been. He watched her unlock her door, then lean across the seat to get his. He started to get in but stopped short when he saw the seat.

"Oh. Just toss those in the back," Jade said, waving a hand at the cassette tapes that littered the passenger seat. "I can never decide what to listen to, so I just bring them all."

Jeremy gathered up the tapes and moved them into the back with a clatter, then slid into his seat. "Um, did Ally tell you employees are supposed to use the lot at the back of the building?" he asked.

Jade shot him an amused smile, her eyes dancing at his expense. "I'm a delicate flower," she said in a matter-of-fact tone. "I can't walk that far."

"Oh . . . I . . . okay," Jeremy said awkwardly. He

knew she was kidding, but for some reason he couldn't come up with a quick response. What was wrong with him? Banter was his thing. He was *always* good at banter. Even with Jessica.

Jade laughed at his lame response, started the car, and pulled out of her space in one quick movement, sending Jeremy's body backward into his seat. Alanis Morrisette instantly blared from the speakers all around him.

"I like it loud," Jade said with a shrug.

"I noticed," Jeremy said. It wasn't clever, but it was something.

"You know," Jade said, taking a corner a little too fast, "I could really go for a burger." Before Jeremy could even decipher what she'd said over all the noise, she had pulled into a drive-through lane behind a blue Volvo. Then she leaned forward slightly, tapping out the beat of the music on the dashboard.

"*Did you forget about me, Mister Du-pli-ci-ty*—I love that line," Jade said, smiling over at him.

"Jade?" Jeremy said, running a hand through his short, brown hair. "Ally told us to get the milk and come right back. What are you doing?"

Jade's black eyes flashed with amusement. "You're so cute when you're panicked," she said with a giggle. Jeremy tried to remain indignant even though his brain was dwelling on the word *cute*.

"Relax, Jeremy. It's no big deal," she said, continuing her little drum session.

Jeremy stared out the front windshield, half wishing he *could* relax and see the excitement in the situation the way Jade seemed to and half wishing she would just bag the burger idea and tell him she was kidding.

"Ally's going to be pissed," he said finally.

Jade shrugged and edged the car up slightly as the line moved. "So we'll tell her the car died, but then you fixed it. That way not only will she not care that we're a little late, but you'll be a hero." Jade grinned an almost irresistible grin. Almost.

"Ally'll never buy that," he told her, shaking his head. "She'll know we're lying."

"Not if *you* tell her," Jade shot back.

Jeremy's eyes narrowed. "What do you mean?"

That one earned a laugh that brought another embarrassed blush to Jeremy's face. "Are you kidding? You're, like, *Responsible Boy* or something," she said, making it sound like the name of a superhero. Jeremy tried not to cringe.

"What makes you say that?" he asked, aware of how geeky his voice sounded.

Jade tilted her head and looked at him the way someone would look at a child who had just said something cute. "It's written all over your face."

Jeremy took a deep breath and stared forward through the windshield. "Park the car," he said firmly.

"What?" Jade asked, excited and amused.

"You heard me," Jeremy said, glancing at her blinding smile. "Park the car. We're going inside to eat."

Jade made a ninety-degree turn and whipped the car into a space, smiling over at him mischievously. "Now, that's more like it."

TIA RAMIREZ

To: adesmond@stanford.edu
From: tee@swiftnet.com
Time: 4:42 P.M.
Subject: what's up?

hey angel,
   how's it going? so do you own the place yet? i'm sure you've been elected president of student government, made a gazillion new friends, and gotten straight a's on all your tests. not to mention you're probably the cutest guy on campus too.
   anyway, things aren't so great here. i've really screwed up this time—i just wish you were at home instead of a couple hundred miles away. none of this ever would have happened if you hadn't left. i really miss you, you know.

   keep in touch.
   love,
   tia

<DELETE MESSAGE>

To: mcdermott@cal.rr.com
From: tee@swiftnet.com
Time: 4:48 P.M.
Subject: what's up?

hey c,
   sorry about this afternoon. i'm just
really stressed out about this whole
mess. you're right, though, we're best
friends—we should be able to hang out and
stuff. it's just that ever since we . . .

<DELETE MESSAGE>

To: lizw@cal.rr.com
From: tee@swiftnet.com
Time: 4:53 P.M.
Subject: what's up?

hi liz,
   i know i'm one of the last people
you want to talk to right now.
probably the last. but do you think
maybe we could meet after school
tomorrow at house of java? i really
want to try to work this out asap.
please?
   let me know,
   tia

<SEND MESSAGE>

Elizabeth Wakefield

To: tee@swiftnet.com
From: lizw@cal.rr.com
Time: 5:18 P.M.
Subject: re: What's up?

Tia,

  I'll meet you at HOJ. 4:30-ish? See
you there.

  Liz

CHAPTER 5
Give Me a Break

"Where have you been?" Ally demanded as Jeremy and Jade stepped into House of Java. Jeremy felt his palms starting to sweat and had to readjust his grip on the plastic bags and milk jugs he was carrying. At least the place wasn't jam-packed with people. Seeing it nearly empty assuaged Jeremy's guilt. Some.

"We, uh . . . ," he began, trying to remember his story. Jade had coached him through it five or six times at Burger Town. "You were just supposed to go to the store for milk," Ally said through clenched teeth. "That should have taken fifteen minutes. You've been gone for forty-five. What happened?"

"The car broke down," Jade jumped in. Ally tilted her head skeptically, narrowing her eyes at the same time. Jeremy could tell she wasn't buying it. He was about to just spill the whole sordid story, onion rings and all, but then Jade leaned toward him almost imperceptibly, bumping the back of his arm with her shoulder.

"It was insane, Ally," he started, the words tumbling

freely from his mouth. "We were on Mellen Drive when Jade's car just quit on us. There was this loud snap, and then it was just like we totally lost power or something. So we—"

"I thought you were taking *your* car," Ally said, folding her arms across her chest.

Jeremy shook his head, reaching up to place the bags on the counter. "Mine's full of football equipment, so we took Jade's instead. Hers had more room." *If you forget about the fact that it's a VW Bug loaded with tapes and old fast-food bags,* Jeremy mused. He was amazed at how easily the lies were flowing now that he had started. And Ally even looked like she was starting to buy it.

"So anyway," Jeremy continued, "we had to pull over on the side of the road. I actually had to push the car to get it out of traffic," he added, glancing over at Jade. She nodded emphatically, her face flushed as if she had just been through the ordeal of her life. *Wow, she's good,* Jeremy thought. "But then when I took a look inside, it was just the fan belt— one of the few things I know how to fix on a car."

Ally opened her mouth, and there was a question in her eyes, but Jade jumped in before Ally could get it out.

"Thank God Jeremy was there," Jade said, grabbing his forearm as if he was her hero. "I don't know what I would have done if it had happened on my way home from work tonight."

Ally nodded slowly. "That is a good thing," she agreed, only a hint of reticence left in her voice. She looked directly into Jeremy's eyes, scrutinizing him. "So how did you fix it?"

Jeremy crossed his arms over his chest. It was time to reel her in. "Something my dad showed me a long time ago," he said, grinning proudly as he approached the only part of the story that actually had some truth to it. "You can replace a fan belt with almost anything as long as it has a little give. It took us a while, but we finally found an old grungy pair of nylons in the backseat of Jade's car." Jeremy felt Jade shift slightly, but she didn't say anything. He almost laughed, knowing that for once he had managed to make *her* uncomfortable. "And I just tied them around the spindles. It's not perfect, but it should last until Jade can get her car into a garage and get a new belt."

"Wow," Ally said, the tight line across her face giving way to an appreciative smile. "I'm impressed. I never would have pegged you for a closet mechanic, Jeremy."

"I think Jeremy's full of surprises," Jade said, grinning up at him. Jeremy felt his face beginning to flush under the weight of her gaze. He tried to hide the internal thrill her attention provoked, but it was difficult when the tiny hairs at the back of his neck were sending shivers down his spine.

"All right," Ally said briskly, returning to business

mode. "The point is you're back, so let's get to work." She came around the front of the counter and picked up the five plastic bags Jade had carried in. "I'll take this milk back to the walk-in. Jeremy, you can grab the rest, and Jade, why don't you take over at the counter?" Having given the orders, Ally disappeared within two seconds, leaving Jeremy and Jade alone. Jeremy let out a long sigh of relief.

Jade whacked his arm with the back of her hand. "Grungy nylons? In *my* backseat? Can you say 'ick'?"

Jeremy laughed. "You've got everything else back there."

"Jeremy!" Ally called from the walk-in refrigerator.

"Duty calls," Jeremy said, grabbing the rest of the milk just as a customer approached the register. Jade trotted around the counter, and Jeremy followed.

"Hey, I had fun," Jeremy whispered as he walked past her, aware that his heart was pounding furiously—although he wasn't sure whether it was from nervousness over his conversation with Ally or the effect being around Jade was having on him.

Jade grinned, her black eyes sparkling. "And that was just the first hour," she said. Then, without missing a beat, she turned to the customer. "What can I get for you?"

Jeremy smiled, keeping his eyes on her as he pushed through the swinging doors to the back room. She had a good point. In one hour he'd broken a slew of his personal rules. He just hoped he could survive the next three.

"So she actually asked you if you wanted to have sex with Conner?" Jessica blurted out, sending tiny flecks of dishwater flying off the pan she had pulled out of the sink. Elizabeth nodded and wiped a tiny soap bubble from her cheek.

"Oops. Sorry," Jessica said.

Elizabeth shrugged and took the pan from Jessica to towel it dry. "Freaky, huh? But I don't know; it was sort of cool. I mean, I think I almost *needed* to talk to her, you know? And I'm glad she knows what's going on now."

"I guess," Jessica said, starting on another pot. She scrubbed at the bottom of it and sighed. "I don't see why we can't just throw these in the dishwasher."

"Don't complain," Elizabeth said, bumping shoulders with her sister. "We're bonding."

"Yeah, right," Jessica scoffed. "I bond better over Ben & Jerry's." She leaned closer to the sink, scrubbing at the pot briskly, then lifting it out to examine it. "Good enough," she said, rinsing it and passing it to Elizabeth. "So," Jessica continued, plunging a glass pan into the dishwater. "What are you going to do about Conner?"

"I don't know," she said slowly. "He wants to talk, but I just . . . I don't know." She lifted the pot Jessica had just finished and stared into it. "Gross," she said, eyeing a big circle of burned-on rice at the bottom. She stepped around her sister and placed the pot back in the pile of dirty dishes.

Jessica scowled. "Perfectionist," she sneered.

"Slacker," Elizabeth returned. Jessica lifted the glass pan, rinsed it, and passed it on to her sister.

"What do you think I should do?" Elizabeth asked.

"I think you should dump him," Jessica said matter-of-factly, punctuating her words by turning on the water full blast.

Elizabeth's fingers clutched the pan as she dried it. "Really?"

"Yeah," Jessica said, scrubbing at the pot in front of her. "Dump him and move on because this whole triangle thing is only going to get messier. Besides, you could do so much better."

But I love him, Elizabeth thought, leaning against the counter. She'd never told her sister about the strength of her feelings for Conner—she'd never even told *him*—but the thought of breaking up with him left her so numb, she could barely even move.

"I don't think I . . ."

Jessica looked up at the tone of Elizabeth's voice and dropped what she was doing. "Wow. You *really* like him, don't you?" she said, her eyes filling with sudden sympathy.

Elizabeth just nodded.

"Okay, then," Jessica said, handing her sister the

pot again. Elizabeth almost dropped it, so Jessica grabbed it back and put it on the dish rack. She rested one hand on the counter and put the other on her hip. "You said you were going to meet Tia at HOJ to talk, right? So if you can't dump him, then you have to tell her to stay away from him."

Elizabeth almost laughed at the mental picture that called up. She and Tia in a catfight in the middle of the quiet little café.

"Right," she said, scoffing. "Like I'm really gonna do that."

"Hey!" Jessica said, her eyes lighting up. "I could do it for you! I could dress up like you and—"

"No! Stop right there," Elizabeth said, standing up straight for the first time in recent memory.

"But I—"

"Nope," Elizabeth countered, holding up her hands. "I think you're right."

Jessica's eyes widened in near comical disbelief. "You do?"

"Yes. I'm going to talk to Tia," Elizabeth said, grabbing a clean towel and rubbing her hands dry. "I don't know if I'm going to give her any orders, but I'll talk to her."

"Good," Jessica said with a quick nod. She went back to the sink and pulled out the drain stopper, causing the obligatory sucking sound as the last of the suds hit the drain. Elizabeth took a deep breath, feeling for the first time like she had an objective.

Until she'd talked to her sister, she hadn't known what she was going to say to Tia, but now she felt better.

Jessica was right—sort of. If Elizabeth wanted to keep Conner, she was going to have to make sure everyone was clear on who meant what to whom. And Tia was as good a place as any to start.

Conner pulled the Mustang into his driveway and cut the engine. All the lights in the house were out except for Megan's room, his mother's room, and the light in the foyer that was always on. There was still a possibility that he could sneak in without being heard. So far, he had been able to put off another confrontation with his mother, and after hanging out at Evan's house until ten-thirty, he was hoping he could do it again.

He tiptoed around the garage and quietly opened the kitchen door. But before he'd even closed it behind him, he realized his luck had run out. His mother was sitting at the kitchen table, her arms folded on the surface and a book facedown in front of her. She had the one small lamp on the table lit.

It was really too bad she couldn't just pass out like she used to.

"It's late," she said, staring at him through the semidarkness.

"Yeah. I'm going to head up to bed," Conner said, starting across the room.

"Hold it," his mother said, extending her arm to block his way. Her voice was forceful but calm. It was a tone Conner had rarely heard over the years, and it caught him off guard. "We've both had plenty of time to cool off. Now it's time we talked this through."

Great, Conner thought, *motherly advice from the absentee mother.*

"Fine," he said coolly. "What do you want? The sordid details?"

Mrs. Sandborn sighed without breaking eye contact. This was new too. A classic disappointed-parent look. Maybe they'd taught her that at rehab.

"Conner—"

"Look, nothing happened, if that's what you're worried about. Not that I expect you to believe me," Conner said, his voice a tired monotone. He adjusted the strap of his backpack on his shoulder, planning to bail as soon as possible. "I went over to Tia's, we watched a movie, and we fell asleep. Then we woke up, and all hell broke loose." He stared at his mother, waiting for her to challenge him.

"I know all that," Mrs. Sandborn said calmly.

It took a good couple of seconds for her words to sink in. "You what?" he asked finally.

"I understand what happened," his mother said, pushing her blond hair behind her ears. Conner was too confused to move. "I *believe* you," she continued, speaking slowly as if to aid his comprehension.

"Did I miss something?" Conner asked.

"I know." Mrs. Sandborn shook her head. "You're not used to having a rational mother. I deserve the stare you're giving me."

Conner's mouth finally snapped shut. "I'm not—"

His mother held up a hand. "But my history aside, we have a problem here, and it has nothing to do with you and Tia," she said. "It's the fact that you come and go around here as you please without so much as a note. Regardless of how things have been in the past, I'm your mother, Conner, and this is *our* home, not a boardinghouse."

Conner rolled his eyes and looked around the room.

Mrs. Sandborn cleared her throat to get his attention, and reluctantly Conner met her gaze. "That's why I'm instituting a curfew," she said.

"A *what?*" Conner spat. "You've got to be kidding. I'm almost eighteen."

"Almost," his mother repeated. "But not quite. From now on, I expect you to be home by nine o'clock on school nights and eleven on the weekends. There may be times that require special exceptions, but I'll expect you to talk to me in advance on those occasions."

"This is a joke," Conner sneered, his entire body going tense. He glared at his mother with contempt, clenching his fists so tightly that his knuckles went white. "You can't be serious. For the last five years

I've been running this place. Picking up groceries, driving Megan around, carting you home when you were sloshed. . . . Now you expect me to start taking orders?" He waited for his mother to blow up and throw it all back at him, but she didn't. Instead she carefully closed her book and tucked it under her arm as she stood.

"I'm going up to bed," she told him, her voice measured. There was the mildest trace of uncertainty—maybe fear—in her eyes, but Conner could tell she was trying to hide it. "If you want to talk to me about this reasonably, I'll be happy to discuss it. In the morning." Then she turned and went upstairs. Conner watched her leave, her forced composure infuriating him even more.

"I don't need this," he muttered under his breath, fishing his car keys out of his pocket and heading for the door.

Curfew, my butt, he thought, wrapping his hand around the doorknob, but something about gripping the cold metal made him stop and think. Just where was he planning to go? To talk to Elizabeth? Tia? Not possible.

He glanced at the clock. He'd left Evan's just a half hour ago, but Evan was on his way to bed then—something about a swim meet tomorrow. And there was no sneaking into Andy's house. His parents were like watchdogs after 10 P.M. The kid wasn't even supposed to get phone calls.

Realizing he was pretty much trapped, Conner let his hand drop from the doorknob and pulled his backpack from his shoulder, throwing it down on the table.

He started to unzip it, but the zipper got stuck halfway. A sudden rage boiled up inside him, and he nearly ripped the fabric when he forced the zipper open. Breathing heavily, his heartbeat pounding in his head, Conner began rifling through his things, retrieving his tattered songbook, a pen, and the two beers he'd swiped from Evan's fridge. Only when he had a firm grasp on the two bottles, dripping with condensation, did he feel his temper begin to subside.

Nothing wrong with a nightcap, he thought, grabbing a bottle opener on his way down to the laundry room. Besides, hadn't his sophomore English teacher told them that Hemingway always drank while he wrote? Conner smiled, popping the top off one of the beers. Then, from some remote corner of his brain, a voice reminded him that Hemingway eventually committed suicide. Conner stared at the two brown bottles as he set them on the wooden table in the basement. *Oh, well,* he thought, snagging one of them and tipping it back to drink. *Not everybody gets a happy ending.*

Conner McDermott

Creative-writing assignment: Love stories typically follow one basic plot: The lovers meet, fall in love, encounter an obstacle, overcome it, and live happily ever after. For Friday's class develop a synopsis for an unconventional love story.

1. Boy meets girl. Girl likes boy. Boy screws it all up. Girl realizes boy is total loser. Girl finds new boy and lives happily ever after. Boy festers in his own misery until he dies.

Even more unconventional:

2. Boy meets girl. Girl likes boy. Boy <u>doesn't</u> screw it all up.

CHAPTER

PARANOIA

"Tia!"

"Hmmm?"

"Tia!"

"I'm sleeping." Tia moaned groggily. She opened her eyes and stared into the darkness, thinking it was the sound of her own voice that had woken her and trying to remember what she had been dreaming about. Then she heard it again.

"Tia. Are you awake?" Someone was whispering from just outside her window.

Conner! Tia thought, throwing back her covers. She tried to peer through the screen, but it was too dark to make out any shapes.

"Meet you at the swings," she whispered, hoping he would hear. Then she ran to her door, grabbed her slippers, and threw on her robe. She was excited, and she wasn't going to let herself feel guilty about it this time. After all, *he* was the one who kept coming to *her*. It wasn't like she was luring him away from Elizabeth or anything. She wasn't even encouraging him.

Tia opened her bedroom door slowly to keep it from squeaking and tiptoed through the kitchen. Then, as silently as possible, she slid open the glass door that led out to the backyard. She had no idea what Conner was going to say to her, but if he even hinted that he might have feelings for her, Tia was going to tell him exactly how she felt. If she could figure it out herself in the next five seconds.

Tia's skin was tingling with anticipation, but when her feet hit the cold brick of the patio, she stopped abruptly. She was definitely losing her mind. *Tell Conner how I* feel? she thought, putting on her slippers. Even that sounded weird.

Still, one thing was clear—she really wanted to see him. Waking up next to Conner and kissing him was the only thing that had felt right since Angel left. And whether it was bad, bizarre, or just plain wrong, Tia wanted to feel it again.

Tia walked toward the swings, peering through the darkness for Conner's shape. When she got closer, she could see him leaning against the slide, silhouetted in the moonlight. *How romantic,* she thought. *How—*

"Andy?" she said. She squinted, but it didn't change the picture before her. "What are you doing here?"

Andy lifted one shoulder. "I just figured, Conner's always sneaking over here to talk—maybe it's time I gave it a try." Tia laughed halfheartedly and stuffed her hands into the pockets of her robe. "I can go," Andy offered, obviously sensing her disappointment.

"No," Tia answered quickly, feeling like a total jerk. "I was just—"

"Expecting someone else?" Andy finished.

"Yeah, I guess," Tia said, walking over and dropping into one of the swings. "Do you know anything about what happened this weekend?" she asked, looking up at him.

Andy nodded and sighed, his breath forming a little fog cloud in the chilly night air. He shuffled over to the other swing and sat down next to her, then pushed off a little, floating back and forth in the blackness. "Conner filled me in."

That was all he was going to tell her. He wasn't going to give her a clue about how Conner felt about it all. Which probably meant Andy thought Tia wouldn't like whatever it was Conner had to say. Tia gripped the swing chains, trying not to let her disappointment show.

"So how are you doing?" Andy asked after a minute.

"Okay," she answered. Even in the dark she could see Andy's expression of doubt. "Okay, I'm *not* okay," she added, turning her swing sideways to face him. "I feel like such a head case, Andy." She leaned forward and looked him directly in the eye. "You have to promise me this never leaves the swing set."

Andy cocked his head, watching her soberly. "Can *I* leave the swing set?" he asked.

"Andy!" Tia snapped, batting him on the shoulder. "This is serious."

"Sorry," he apologized, chuckling slightly. He rubbed his face, as if he was trying to contort it into a more sober expression, then nodded and cleared his throat.

Tia wrapped her arms around the chains of her swing and let her knees rock from side to side, twisting herself back and forth. "Okay, so . . . this is going to sound really stupid, but I think I might . . . *like* Conner. You know, as more than a friend," she added, staring down at her fidgeting hands.

She sensed Andy sitting up a little straighter and knew he was trying hard not to tell her all the reasons why she couldn't be with Conner. The three of them had been friends for so long, and Tia wasn't oblivious to the effects this would have on Andy. She knew that if she and Conner ever did get together, things would change between the three of them.

Again the thought of her and Conner as a couple was so odd, it sent a chill down her spine. She wrapped her arms around herself and pressed her legs together to try to warm up and control the shakes.

"He didn't . . . say anything like that about me, did he?" Tia asked, glancing at Andy quickly. His face said it all, and her heart dropped.

95

"Sorry, Tee," he said in a pitiful tone that made her want to cringe.

"I'm such a loser!" Tia said, kicking at the ground with the toe of her fuzzy red slipper. Why was she doing this to herself? Why would any girl in her right mind even want to get near Conner the heart smasher?

Andy was quiet for a minute. Then he shuffled his feet across the ground, moving his swing closer to hers until he bumped her. Tia looked up reluctantly.

"You're not a loser," Andy said, his brown eyes serious. "Losers don't have cool friends like me who show up outside their windows at 2 A.M. to go swinging."

Tia pulled her long hair back from her face and twisted it, letting it tumble down her back in a messy coil. "I think that might make us both losers," she said, slumping slightly. "Got any other words of wisdom I can't stop you from sharing?"

"How much time do you have?" Andy asked, jerking his swing sideways to dodge another blow to his shoulder.

"Jerk," Tia muttered, aware that her mood was lightening in spite of Andy's bad jokes. Or possibly because of them.

Andy twisted his swing around several times, then lifted his feet, sending himself into a spiral that rapidly picked up speed. "Tee, you can't really be serious about liking Conner," he said, his voice alternating between loud and soft as he spun toward her and then away again.

"Why not?" Tia asked.

When Andy's swing came to a stop, he stared straight ahead, looking confused, and planted his feet on the ground.

"Ugh. That always seems like it's going to be so fun until I do it," he said. Tia smirked and waited for him to regain his composure. "Where was I?" he asked.

"Why I don't want Conner," Tia supplied, staring past him at the pink blossoms that were somehow still in full bloom despite a couple of nights' worth of frost.

"Right," Andy answered, snapping his fingers. "Conner's just so . . . somber and stuff. I mean, have you ever listened to his song lyrics? People suck, the world sucks, we're all just going to die anyway," he mocked. "If you started dating him, you'd have to start dressing all in pink just to counteract his moods, and frankly, it's just not your color."

"Come on," Tia said, swinging from side to side. "Conner's not *that* bad." She bumped Andy, jostling his swing. "And I do too look good in pink."

"You just keep telling yourself that," Andy said, scratching at the back of his neck. "Anyway, even though Conner is basically a good guy, there's just something karmically wrong about starting a relationship with someone who used to pee in your parents' flower beds."

Tia giggled, glancing at the flowers again. "We were only four, Andy," she said.

"I know," Andy returned, keeping a straight face even as Tia swung toward him again. "But come on, that's got to be a turnoff."

Tia laughed again, stopping her swing right next to Andy's and leaning over to kiss him on the cheek. "You're the best, you know?" she said. "You always know how to cheer me up."

"It's a gift," Andy said offhandedly, but Tia sensed he was blushing.

She let herself swing back to the center, then planted her feet on the ground, looking up at the half-moon. "You're so right," she said firmly. "When you really think about it, I already know enough about Conner to know it would never work." She sighed, watching the moisture of her breath dance up into the air. "I don't know what I was thinking. . . . Except he's really hot," she added mischievously.

"Pardon me while I vomit," Andy said, scrunching up his face.

Tia laughed, tilting her head forward so that her hair fell around her face. "Thanks for coming over, Andy," she said, rising from her swing. "It was really sweet of you to check in on me."

"Oh, uh . . . yeah," Andy said, standing as well. He

glanced around the yard as if he wasn't quite sure where to go.

"That *is* why you came over, isn't it?" Tia asked. "I mean, I just assumed . . ."

Tia trailed off, realizing she never really *had* asked Andy why he was here. She'd just monopolized the conversation as usual. She wanted to slap herself for being so inconsiderate. "Andy, was there something you wanted to talk to me about?" she asked, studying his face, half shadowed in the darkness.

Andy immediately looked away, bringing his hands together in front of himself and picking at something underneath one of his fingernails. "No, that was it. I just wanted to make sure you were okay," he answered quickly.

Tia narrowed her eyes. "Are you sure?"

"Why else would I be in your backyard at—" Andy checked his watch. "Whoa—almost 3 A.M.," he finished. "I better get going. I have to get up in a couple of hours." He just looked at her for a moment, as if he was expecting her to say something else, but Tia had no idea what he wanted. "Well, see ya," he said, turning on his heel. He started toward the break in the hedges at the rear of the yard, but Tia didn't move. He was walking funny. And his posture was all stiff. Something was definitely up.

"Andy?" she said, feeling a wave of sudden concern.

He turned around quickly, as if he'd just heard a gunshot. "Yeah?"

"I just want to make sure you don't have any personal secrets you wanted to divulge." She watched for him to flinch or blink or sigh, but Andy just chuckled.

"You wish," he said, sounding a little flat. "Sorry, but you're the only one with secret longings around here tonight."

"Loser," Tia said with a smile.

"Moron," Andy shot back, grinning for real.

"Thanks again," Tia said, backing toward the house.

"Yeah, you'd better get your beauty rest," Andy said, backing up himself. "You need it."

Tia just rolled her eyes and lifted her hand in a wave, then turned and slipped into the kitchen. Once inside, she realized she felt a million times lighter than she had most of the day. Andy was right. The idea of a Tia-and-Conner matchup was ridiculous. They had known each other too long and been through too much. They'd probably kill each other if they tried to get any closer. Suddenly, in the darkness, everything looked perfectly clear.

Problem was, she had to convince Elizabeth, Jessica, Conner, and the rest of the student body that there was nothing to gossip or worry about. Tia sighed and shuffled off to her room.

Forget about beauty rest. If today was anything

like yesterday, she was going to need the next three hours of sleep just to survive.

As Elizabeth fumbled with her lock on Tuesday morning, she felt like a huge bull's-eye was hanging on her back. Like any second someone was going to swoop down on her and cause some more emotional stress. There was nothing she wanted more than just to go unnoticed. She opened her locker door quickly, intending to unload the books from her backpack and take off for the bathroom until the bell rang. Instead her eyes were immediately drawn to a piece of cardboard that had been wedged into one of the vents.

It was bright orange with pieces of dark blue lettering, and as soon as she started unfolding it, Elizabeth knew it had been torn from an old box of laundry detergent. *Conner*. She smiled, picturing him hanging out alone in the basement laundry room. A strange sense of nostalgia tugged at her heart as she remembered one night when they'd gotten into a debate down there about literature. She'd wanted him so much then and thought she'd never have him.

Everything had changed so much . . . and not at all.

She flipped over the cardboard to see that the plain brown side was marked with his unmistakable handwriting, and her heart fluttered with nervousness. She was almost too scared to read it. But she couldn't stop herself either.

waiting.
seconds passing like days.
words echoing in slow motion.
time all but standing still,
but still—
waiting.

Elizabeth read the poem three times, her heart pounding hard. It wasn't until she started to feel slightly dizzy that she realized she'd been holding her breath the whole time. She exhaled slowly and leaned back against the locker next to hers, the relief washing over her as the breath sank out.

He'd gone out on a limb for her, writing this. And Conner wasn't a person who went out on limbs. He pretty much avoided limbs at all costs.

She ran her fingers over the ink, imagining him sitting down there, on top of the rickety table, his legs splayed out in front of him, concentrating on his little piece of ripped box. Part of her just wanted to go find him right then. She had the sudden, uncontrollable urge to tell him she loved him and to tell him she believed there was nothing going on between him and Tia.

She swung her locker shut and started down the hall but then stopped so quickly, she almost caused a collision. Stepping toward the wall and out of the crowd, Elizabeth took a deep breath and tried to calm down. If she talked to him now, she would only be following her heart. And if she did that, she would definitely get hurt again. She was going to have to think this through first.

Slowly she turned and went back to her locker. It was time to start functioning like a normal human being. And that meant actually taking out the books she needed for class before she ran to homeroom. But when she was standing in front of the open locker, she couldn't even recall her morning classes.

She held up the jagged cardboard and studied the poem again, fingering the square's torn edges delicately. *Just go,* she thought, squeezing her eyes shut.

"No," she answered herself firmly. This was ridiculous. One little poem and she was ready to forgive everything.

Elizabeth stuck the cardboard back in the vent where she had found it and grabbed her AP history books instead. Then, before she had time to change her mind, she slammed the locker shut and started down the hall. But after about ten feet she turned quickly and shuffled back, groaning at her own weakness.

She popped open the locker, grabbed the poem, and stuffed it into the front pocket of her jeans. Okay. So maybe it wasn't a good time to talk to Conner, but he did go through a lot of trouble to write the poem for her. It would be rude to leave it behind.

*   *   *

Tia watched the clock on Ms. Dalton's wall, convinced that time was actually moving backward. She could have sworn that the minute hand hadn't moved a millimeter in the last five minutes. And this was the last place she would ever want to get caught in a time warp.

Ms. Dalton had given the French class fifteen minutes of group time to work on their upcoming skits, and Tia was stuck with Amy Sutton and Annie Whitman, two girls from the cheerleading squad who had opted to use the time to finish a physics lab instead. They'd asked Tia if she minded, but she didn't care. She couldn't concentrate anyway.

To her right Elizabeth, Maria, and Jessica were working together, and every time they spoke—in French *or* English—Tia got a sick feeling in her stomach, convinced that they were talking about her like she was the scum of the earth. But on her left things were just as bad. Melissa and her group were whispering, giggling, and passing notes back and forth. Tia looked up at the clock again.

Come on! Move! she commanded, slumping forward in her chair. She was just about ready to give up and put her head down when she heard Melissa whispering again and was positive that she had heard her own name. Tia glanced over, but Melissa's entire group suddenly seemed to be hard at work. Tia blew a puff of air toward her forehead. She was probably just being paranoid. Besides, how could

Melissa possibly know anything? It wasn't like she and Conner were best buddies, and she definitely wasn't on speaking terms with Jessica or Elizabeth. And if Melissa knew anything, it would be all over school by now. There was no way she would keep something this juicy to herself.

"*D'accord,*" said Ms. Dalton. "*Retournez au grand groupe, s'il vous plaît.*"

Finally, Tia thought, turning her desk to the front again. She listened to the sound of metal scraping the tiled floor as everyone else did the same. *This should eat up five minutes,* she thought while Ms. Dalton tried to call the class to order again.

"*Attention, s'il vous plaît!*" she called, and the room quieted down a bit. "*Nous avons commencé un nouveau livre aujourd'hui. Un script.*"

A play? Tia wondered. *Is that what she said?*

Her guess was confirmed when Ms. Dalton began handing out the books. Tia couldn't see the title, but the way the pages were bound, it definitely looked like a script. Tia brightened a little. She liked reading aloud in an exaggerated French accent, and plays always made class time fly by. She was starting to feel a little better—at least about the rest of French class— when she heard Melissa laughing again.

Tia's stomach fluttered, but she tried to ignore it. She knew she was way too sensitive right now to take any of her gut reactions seriously. It wasn't even like there was anything for Melissa to know. After all, she and Conner were still just friends, and no one—except for Andy—had any clue that there might be more to it. Tia sighed and ran her fingers through the back of her hair. If she didn't stop psychoanalyzing everything, she was going to make herself crazy. Still, when she saw Melissa's hand shoot up, Tia's entire body tensed.

"Madame Dalton?" Melissa called from the corner. There was something smug in her voice—a tone Tia recognized all too well. *"Je crois que Tia devrait être Emma."* Tia bristled at the mention of her name.

What did she say, what did she say? Tia asked herself, combing through her French vocabulary. Devrait . . . *that's a form of* devoir, *which is* . . . should *or* ought. *She thinks I should be Emma?* Tia wondered. What did that mean?

Oh, in the play, she realized, reaching forward as Amy passed a stack of scripts to her. She snatched hers quickly and passed the rest back to Annie, determined to figure out what Melissa was talking about. Tia flipped her book over urgently, and as soon as she saw the title, her stomach dropped.

It was an adaptation of *Madame Bovary.* Tia and Melissa had both read it in English class at El Carro last year. Tia's pulse quickened as she listened to the sound of Melissa's giggling over her shoulder and realized that Elizabeth, Maria, and Jessica were all staring at her too. Melissa had just volunteered Tia for the role of Emma Bovary—the adulteress.

Andy Marsden

Reasons why I'm glad I didn't spill my thoughts to Tia, even though I wasn't necessarily <u>planning</u> on it when I went over there at two o'clock in the morning:

1. She's delusional. She wants Conner, who is so obviously in love with Elizabeth and is so obviously scared of that and is so obviously finding the worst way to screw it up. And she thinks she looks good in pink. 'Nuff said.

2. When she doesn't know what to say, she babbles. And I was getting a little tired anyway. I couldn't have stuck around for that.

3. Okay, she is my best friend, but she's going through a little self-absorption thing right now. Which is fine. Everyone has to do that every once in a while. I just don't want to say, "I'm gay," and have the response be, "That's nice. Now, about me and Conner . . ."

4. The girl is so obsessed with everyone finding love and being part of a couple, she'd be scouring the streets for a boyfriend for me in seconds. Which I am definitely not ready for.

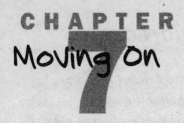
"Wait a second," Jeremy said incredulously. "You've been to Paris, London, Milan, Rome, *and* Madrid?" He ripped open a brown paper wrapper, pulling out a stack of small, white napkins. "That must have been unbelievable."

Jade took the napkins from him and shrugged. "Yeah, it was a cool summer, but I didn't really get to see that much," she said, turning a silver napkin holder on its side and pressing the napkins into it. "I went with this touring-teen-dance-company thing, and our chaperons were like wardens. They never let us go anywhere fun." She righted the holder, setting it at the far edge of the counter, and turned to Jeremy for another handful of napkins. But Jeremy was just standing there, shaking his head.

"Did you see the Eiffel Tower?" he asked, raising his eyebrows.

Jade rolled her eyes. "Yep."

"And Big Ben?" he prompted.

"Yep."

"The Coliseum?"

She sighed. "Yep."

Jeremy handed her another stack of napkins. "Oh, yeah, you did nothing fun," he said sarcastically. He would have given anything to see the world like that. Back when his family had money, his dad took them to the same two places every year—Vail at Christmas and St. Bart's in the spring. He wasn't complaining, but even those places got boring when they became too familiar.

"Buildings," Jade said, stuffing the napkins into the next empty holder. "Whoopee." Her tone was so flat, she could have been talking about logarithms.

"Okay," Jeremy said, leaning back against the counter and crossing his arms over his chest. "What would you consider a good time in a foreign land?"

Jade's eyes sparkled as she slapped the napkin holder shut. "Meeting foreign boys," she said with a grin.

"Oh," Jeremy said, blushing like a tomato and staring down at the tiled floor.

Jade laughed, tossing her hair off her face. "You are *so* cute," she said. Then she reached across in front of him to grab a new package of napkins, coming so close, they could have been slow dancing. As her hand brushed his shoulder, he caught a whiff of her exotic-smelling shampoo. It practically gave him a head rush.

"Cute, huh?" he said, grinning uncontrollably.

"Definitely," Jade replied, staring up into his eyes.

Jeremy felt his blush deepen. He'd never known a girl who was so forward and fearless. He kinda liked it. It made him want to be reckless too. All he wanted to do in that moment was lean forward and kiss her. And he would have too. If they weren't at work.

The bell above the door jingled, effectively squelching the moment. Jeremy looked up to see Jessica and Elizabeth walking into the café. His brow furrowed. Jessica wasn't supposed to work until four-thirty. He glanced down at his watch. It was twenty-five after four! Time sure flew when he was around Jade.

"Hey, guys!" Jessica said, stepping right up to the counter and leaning her forearms on the surface. Elizabeth hung back, surveying the café and keeping an eye on the front door.

Jeremy turned around to face her, and Jade stepped up next to him, still keeping only the minutest amount of space between his hip and hers. His hyperawareness of her presence sent shivers down Jeremy's spine. He tried to focus.

"Hey, Jess," he said. "How's it—"

"It's a good thing you're here, Jessica," Jade interrupted, holding her palm at the side of her mouth, as if she didn't want Jeremy to overhear. "I haven't been able to do a thing with him all afternoon," she said, darting her eyes toward Jeremy.

"Very funny," Jeremy said, scowling down at her.

"Come on," Jade chided him. "Take it like a man."

She laughed and bumped him with her hip. Jeremy couldn't have wiped the grin off his face if he tried.

"Do you see the kind of abuse I have to take from her?" he joked, but Jessica didn't seem to be laughing. Instead she seemed to be focusing on the lack of space between him and Jade.

Suddenly self-conscious, Jeremy pushed away from the counter and took a step back, shoving his hands in his back pockets. "I'm telling you, it's brutal," he said, his voice cracking slightly as he inched away.

Jessica smiled. "Yeah, but you probably deserve it," she said. Jeremy thought he detected a slight edge to her voice, but he couldn't be sure. She held his gaze for a minute, raising her eyebrows slightly before she looked away. Jeremy felt his shoulders tense.

"He does," Jade jumped in. "He's been screwing up orders all afternoon, and he keeps trying to blame it on me just because I'm new."

"Whatever," Jeremy said. "You—"

"I know what you mean," Jessica interrupted. She moved farther down the counter so that she was directly in front of Jade and started talking as if Jeremy weren't even there. "He did the same thing to me when I started, and he kept bossing me around like he actually knew what he was doing. It's pathetic, really."

"Tell me about it," Jade said, leaning in toward her friend. "Yesterday when we were—"

"All right, all right," Jeremy said, stepping forward and waving his hand between the two of them. "We'll be working together for the next three hours. Can't you wait five minutes to start in on the Jeremy bashing? I mean, Jessica hasn't even punched in yet."

"That's true," Jade said matter-of-factly, standing up straight. "If we're going to spend our time swapping Jeremy stories, you might as well be getting paid."

"Good point," Jessica agreed, heading for the time clock.

Jade started to straighten up a mess she'd made earlier by the espresso machine. As she moved away from him, Jeremy took a deep breath. The spine-tingling pleasure he'd felt moments ago was quickly supplanted by a strange feeling of guilt. It was a much less pleasurable feeling.

Was Jessica jealous of Jade? Was it actually remotely possible that she could still . . . want him?

In his periphery Jeremy thought he caught Jessica staring at him, but when he looked again, she was involved in a conversation with Elizabeth. Jeremy rubbed the back of his neck and waited, but Jessica didn't even glance in his direction. Great. Now he was imagining things.

Still, he couldn't help thinking that he should try to tone down the flirting a bit when he, Jade, and Jessica were working together. Maybe everyone would just be more comfortable.

But why? a little voice inside him asked. Jessica was the one who had ended things. And she had even gone so far as to tell him she wasn't interested in anything more than a friendship.

Jeremy turned back to Jade, who was pouring milk and cream into the large silver carafes at the serving station. He loved the way her hair hung forward, accentuating her sharp jawline. And the way she smirked every time she caught him watching her. She was fun to be with—why should he feel guilty for being attracted to her?

Besides, it wasn't like he had any obligations to Jessica. She had taken care of that when she had chosen Will. So what was he waiting for? He glanced over at Jessica one more time. She had moved on, so why shouldn't he? Jeremy smiled as he grabbed a bag of sugar packets and went to help Jade.

It was time to forget about the past and live in the now. Maybe he would even get a chance to ask Jade out tonight.

Conner was holding on to his sanity by a thread. He'd been out of school for less than two hours, and already he'd laced into his sister for no apparent reason, torn twenty pages out of his songbook, and run a stop sign, earning a hefty ticket from a policewoman who just happened to be sitting around the corner.

I've got to get a grip, he told himself, swinging open

the glass door at HOJ and causing the loudest bell clanging ever made in the small café from the force of his push. None of what had happened in the last couple of hours even remotely compared to the day he'd had at school. Tia and Elizabeth had both completely ignored him—even after he'd left Elizabeth that poem. He'd been sure she was going to come back to him. That was exactly the kind of thing that would get her attention. But no. Nothing. And Tia had somehow become the master of the cold shoulder. She hadn't even *looked* at him once.

Conner glanced at the counter warily and was relieved to find Jade Wu—not Jessica Wakefield—behind the counter. Maybe his luck was starting to turn.

Stepping up to the counter, Conner checked out the brews-of-the-day board. Maybe he would try something other than his normal superstrong black coffee. Maybe he'd even put some milk in it or something. A novel idea. He glanced over at the self-serve counter to check out the choices, and that was when he saw them.

Tia and Elizabeth. Sitting together. *Talking* to each other.

Conner's fists immediately clenched. What the hell was going on? He must be hallucinating. Conner narrowed his eyes, but they were still there, hanging out in a couple of overstuffed chairs by the window. And judging by the expressions on their faces, they were having a pretty intense conversation.

Lovely, Conner thought, crumpling the five-dollar bill in his hand into a tiny ball. *No one's even acknowledging me, but they can get together for a cup of coffee?*

"Uh, Conner? Can I get you something?" Jade asked from someplace very far away. The anger spinning inside his head almost drowned her out. His brain was too busy formulating the perfect line—the perfect words to spit out when he stalked over there and told them exactly what he thought of their little powwow.

Of course, for the first time in his life, he came up blank.

"Conner?" Jade repeated. Conner faced her, focusing all of his energy into clenching his jaw in an effort to restrain himself from freaking at an innocent bystander.

"Forget it. Coffee's not what I need right now," he muttered. Then he turned and stormed out before Elizabeth or Tia had a chance to notice that he had ever come in.

"So, I'm really glad you showed up," Tia said, taking a sip from her coffee and setting it back on the small table between her and Elizabeth.

She kissed my boyfriend, Elizabeth thought, staring at Tia's mouth as she talked. *She kissed Conner. She kissed Conner.*

Every time her brain repeated those three little

words, it was like another stab wound in Elizabeth's chest. And every time she felt the stabbing, her anger deepened. She had no idea what she was thinking coming here. There was no way this was going to be a rational discussion.

"I almost didn't," Elizabeth said flatly. It came out sounding bitchy, but she didn't care. *I wonder if he touched her face when he kissed her like he does mine,* she thought, her stomach turning at the thought of those rough fingertips touching someone else's skin.

"Oh," Tia faltered, retrieving her coffee stirrer from the napkin on the table and tapping it nervously against her palm. "Well, still, I think it's good that you did. I mean, I'm hoping we can get this whole mess straightened out before it gets totally out of hand, you know?"

Elizabeth narrowed her eyes. As far as she was concerned, the situation was already out of hand. She couldn't trust one of her best friends, and she had no idea whether or not to stay with a guy who could possibly be the love of her life.

"What exactly do you want to straighten out?" Elizabeth asked, leaning back in her chair and placing her arms on the armrests. "I mean, you've already told me everything that happened—*right?*"

There was no way she actually wanted an answer to that question.

"Well, yeah . . . of course," Tia sputtered, concentrating on her hands. "I mean, there was just the . . .

you know, *kiss* Saturday morning, and it's not like anything's happened since then. Or like anything ever happened *before*," she added quickly.

Elizabeth squirmed slightly in her seat. The girl was babbling. Was she hiding something? What if she and Conner had already talked and gotten their stories straight so they'd know what to tell her? If they were talking about her behind her back, Elizabeth would be beyond humiliated.

She took a deep breath to try to calm her nerves, but it didn't work. Forget kissing. Even the thought of these two *talking* made her ill.

"He cares about you, Liz," Tia said quickly. "He really does, I know it. I mean, he's never been serious about anyone before, and I would know—we *are* best friends. But that's all we are."

"Right," Elizabeth scoffed. She was trying to protect herself, but she wanted so badly to believe what Tia was saying.

"Seriously," Tia continued, shifting in her seat. "That kiss was a major fluke—think about it. Conner and I have known each other since we were kids, so he's had, like, ten years to say or do something to show that he wanted more than a friendship with me, but he never did. *You're* the one he broke all of his stupid rules for—not me."

Elizabeth felt a tiny smile playing about her lips. Tia was right about that. She was the first person Conner had serious feelings for. She knew that. But something about the way Tia was delivering her message bothered Elizabeth. It was like she didn't really want to say what she was saying.

Elizabeth squinted, eyeing Tia's fingers as they busily bent the coffee stirrer into a series of crooked angles. She seemed so nervous. *And why won't she look up at me?* Elizabeth wondered. These were not good signs.

Could Jessica be right? Should she really demand that Tia and Conner stay away from each other? Deep down, Elizabeth knew she had no right to do such a thing—knew that if anyone asked her to do it, she'd laugh in that person's face. But at that moment she couldn't think of any other way she'd ever feel secure again.

"Listen—"

Tia's tired brown eyes widened hopefully, and Elizabeth's mouth snapped shut. She couldn't do it. There was no way she could be that unreasonable. But there was something she had to know.

"Tia . . ." Elizabeth hesitated, clasping her hands together. "I know you said there's nothing going on between you and Conner, but . . ." Elizabeth took a deep breath, unable to believe what she was about to say. Somehow she managed to look Tia in the eye. "Do you, um, *like* Conner?"

Tia's eyes darkened ever so slightly. Then she blinked and looked down at the floor.

Elizabeth's stomach dropped so fast, it felt like it

was being sucked through a straw. It was all the answer she needed, but Tia was talking anyway.

"Uh, well." She hesitated, running a hand through her hair. "I don't . . . I guess I'm . . . not really sure."

She might as well have slammed a fork into Elizabeth's heart.

"I'm sure we don't belong together, though," Tia added quickly.

But Elizabeth barely heard her. So much for honesty is the best policy. All around her, voices seemed to be getting louder. Other people's boisterous conversations and laughter filled the air, and the room seemed to be getting darker. Elizabeth tried to focus on her coffee cup, but it kept blurring.

"Liz? Are you okay?" Tia asked, leaning across the table and lightly touching Elizabeth's wrist. Elizabeth carefully moved her arm away from Tia's hand, trying to make the gesture appear casual by brushing back a strand of hair. All the while her mind was swimming. If Tia had suddenly realized that she might like Conner, wasn't it just as likely that Conner might like her? And Tia and Conner had always been so close. If this thing between them had always been there—even if it was just in the background, then . . .

Then Conner was never really mine, Elizabeth thought, tears welling up in her eyes.

Elizabeth cleared her throat and blinked several times to hold back the waterworks. It only served to make them worse.

"Um, yeah, I'm fine," she said, her voice cracking in spite of her effort to keep it level. She carefully brought her hand to her neck, fingering the silver choker that Conner had always fidgeted with whenever he had his arm around her. "I just—" Her voice was so raspy, she had to stop and clear her throat again. She tried hard to regain her composure, but the room felt like it was closing in on her. "I have to go," she said, planting her feet on the floor in front of her chair.

"No, wait," Tia said, leaning forward. "I haven't even had a chance to explain everything." Tia looked like a puppy dog, begging her not to leave.

But Elizabeth couldn't imagine what else there was to explain. It was obvious to her now that Tia was closer to Conner than she could ever be. And that Tia knew things about him that Elizabeth would never know. She needed an escape route. She turned and checked the counter for Jessica, but her sister was nowhere in sight.

Elizabeth stood and felt her knees starting to buckle beneath her. She placed her hand on the top of her chair to steady herself. "I'm just gonna go to the bathroom," she said, mostly to herself. "I have to . . . think for a second."

Tia asked her if she was okay again, but Elizabeth ignored her. She had to get out of the room and figure out what to do. She knew for sure that it was time to take charge of her life.

She just had no idea how to do it.

Jessica Wakefield

Okay, Ally left me next week's schedule so that I could go over it and see how it's done. Fine. No problem.

Except that the woman is insane.

Every single shift Jade is working, she's working with Jeremy.

Every one.

I mean, <u>come on!</u> The girl's new. She needs to be trained. But should that responsibility constantly fall on Jeremy? I mean, Ally's the one who told him to get a life, and now she has him practically <u>mentoring</u> the rookie. He can't be expected to do that all by himself — work so closely with her and hold her hand through every little thing. I mean, imagine how _frustrating_ that would be!

For a second I thought about redoing the schedule. As a manager, I am allowed to do that. But I don't want to step on Ally's toes my first week on the job. I am, however, going to offer to do _next_ week's schedule.

I mean, _someone_ should be looking out for Jeremy around here, right?

CHAPTER 8
It's Only Tuesday

Okay, what *did I just do?* Tia wondered, leaning back in her chair, feeling completely numb. She hadn't actually just told Elizabeth that she might like Conner, had she? It sort of defeated the whole purpose of being here in the first place.

"To work things out," Tia muttered, trying to get her brain back on track. "You were supposed to be here to work things out."

She leaned back her head and gazed up at the slowly turning ceiling fan above. It seemed to be mocking her—going around so lazily while her insides were busy doing the Mexican hat dance. Elizabeth had to hate her guts right now. What was she going to say when she got back from the bathroom?

Tia let out a long, slow sigh. Maybe she'd come back and say Tia could have him. She'd say, *"You guys have been friends for so long, and I can't come between you. So I'm just going to step aside and—"*

Shaking her head, Tia chuckled at herself. Yeah, right. Like *that* would ever happen.

"There you go, laughing again. *Now* are you going to tell me what's so funny?"

Tia's head snapped up at the sound of Elizabeth's voice. But it didn't really sound like Elizabeth at all. It sounded a lot more firm. And a lot more mean.

"Nothing!" Tia said, staring up at her friend. Elizabeth was hovering next to Tia's chair, and her normally laughing bright blue-green eyes seemed to have turned to steel. Her whole body was as rigid as a stack of bricks. Tia's stomach flopped quickly. So much for the amicable stepping aside she'd been imagining.

"Nothing's funny," Tia said, bringing her legs up onto her chair and turning in her seat to face Elizabeth. "I was just . . . thinking, and I—"

Elizabeth squeezed her eyes shut and held up one hand. "You know what? Forget it," she said quickly. "There's just something I have to say, and I have to say it fast before I lose my nerve."

"Okay," Tia said quietly.

"I want you to stay away from Conner," Elizabeth said.

"What!" Tia spat immediately. The whole room was reeling, and she saw a few people look up in their direction. It didn't matter in the slightest. Elizabeth had apparently lost her mind. "You can't tell me what to do," Tia said, planting her feet on the floor and standing up straight. She was still a few inches shorter than Elizabeth, but she didn't care. No one was going to decide who she could and couldn't be friends with.

"Tia," Elizabeth said, almost pleadingly. "I don't want to get into a big thing with you, but put yourself in my place. How am I supposed to ever be comfortable around you guys again?"

"That's your problem, not mine," Tia fumed, grabbing her bag and slinging it over her shoulder. "God, Liz! I came here to try to save our friendship, and this is what you do?"

She was about to turn on her heel and stalk away, but Elizabeth's eyes flashed, and the anger there made Tia pause. "You said it yourself," Elizabeth said. "Conner really cares about me. If I go to him right now and tell him he can have either you or me, who do you really think he'll pick?"

Tia couldn't believe what she was hearing. Had Elizabeth grown a backbone while she was in the bathroom? And why did her words bring out every hidden insecure cell in Tia's body?

Because deep down, you know she's right, Tia answered herself. *Conner loves her. She may not know that for sure, but you do. You've known that for a long time.*

"You wouldn't," Tia said finally. Her voice was barely a whisper. "You would never."

"Yeah?" Elizabeth said, picking up her own bag. She looked Tia in the eye as she rolled back her shoulders. "Well, I never thought you'd kiss my boyfriend either."

And with that, Elizabeth pushed through the front door and disappeared into the crowded street. Tia slowly lowered herself back into her chair, staring at the nearly full coffee mugs on the table.

"There's no way that just happened," she whispered to herself.

"Oh, it did," Jessica said from about three feet away. She was standing, looking proudly out the windows at the street. "I just never knew my sister had it in her."

"I can't believe you." Jeremy shook his head at Jade. He was, of course, smiling. Jessica couldn't help but notice that he *always* seemed to be smiling when Jade was in his line of vision. Jessica stared at them from behind the counter, where she was straightening the already meticulously arranged coffee mugs.

Jade paused in her table wiping and put one hand on her hip. "He's the one who gave me the lame pickup line," she shot back, gesturing toward the exit, where a somewhat attractive, thirtyish man was slinking out of the café.

"I know," Jeremy said. He picked up a cup and saucer and dumped them into the plastic busing bin. "But you totally shot him down. I mean, 'you could be my father'? That was harsh."

"True, but that's Jade," Jessica whispered to herself. If Jeremy didn't like her bluntness, maybe he should stop flirting with her so much. Jessica watched them out of the corner of her eye, flinching when she saw the way he was looking at Jade. It was the same admiring look he used to bestow on her, and every time she saw it directed at her friend, Jessica felt like something was tearing at her stomach. She picked up a mug and set it down abruptly, knocking it against another one.

The happy soon-to-be couple glanced over at her. "Sorry," Jessica called cheerily.

Jade furrowed her brow and turned back to Jeremy. "Well, he *could* have been my father. I was just pointing out the obvious," she said with a shrug. "And besides, forty-year-olds should not be coming on to high-school girls. He's obviously got a problem." *He wasn't forty,* Jessica thought, exhaling sharply.

"Come on, he wasn't forty," Jeremy said, bringing a quick smile to Jessica's face. "Maybe thirty, tops."

Jade walked by Jeremy slowly, eyeing him up and down. "Let's just say I prefer guys closer to my own age," she said with a flirtatious grin.

"Oh, please," Jessica snapped, squeezing her eyes shut as she realized she had said it aloud. Jade and Jeremy stared at her. "I—I can't get these mugs to stay where I want them," she stammered, managing a weak smile.

Talk about lame, she thought.

Jeremy and Jade exchanged a look, then started talking again, more quietly this time.

That's right, Jessica thought, turning to the sink and flipping the water on to rinse out a filter. *Go back to your love fest—don't mind me.*

She glanced over her shoulder and saw Jeremy blushing, which was just so cringe worthy, Jessica thought she was going to barf. Then Jeremy said something that Jessica couldn't quite hear, and Jade touched his arm, giggling. Jessica slammed a few dishes around in the sink, unable to believe what she was seeing. Jade knew she and Jeremy used to be a couple. How could she just keep flirting with him like that when Jessica was only ten feet away? "Hey! I have an idea!" Jade said suddenly. "Maybe Ally needs some milk!"

"We should call ahead to Burger Town, then," Jeremy answered, causing them to both burst out laughing. What was that about? Jessica watched Jeremy grinning from ear to ear, his excitement almost unbearable. But why was he acting so ridiculous around Jade? She wasn't even his type . . . was she?

"Hey, Jess," Jeremy said, approaching her as she attempted to look busy. "I think Jade and I are going to grab a couple of coffees and take a break while it's slow. Is that cool?"

Would it matter if I said no? Jessica thought bitterly. "Yeah, that's fine," she said, trying to sound relaxed. "I wanted to sweep up back here anyway," she lied.

"Great, thanks," Jeremy said, smiling as he waved for Jade to join him.

"Don't worry, Jess," Jade said as she ducked behind the counter and whipped up a couple of regular coffees. "I'll keep my eye on the clock and make sure it's only a fifteen-minute break. I know what a slacker Jeremy is."

"Hey," Jeremy called back, pretending to be offended, but Jade just giggled again and smiled at Jessica before heading over to the table Jeremy had picked. The one farthest away from Jessica.

"Ha, ha, ha," Jessica whispered to herself as she grabbed the broom from the storage closet. *I swear, if I have to hear that laugh one more time . . .* She jabbed at the tiled floor with the broom, sending pulses of anger down the wooden handle and out through the bristles with each stroke. Why was this bothering her so much anyway? She'd thought she was over Jeremy. She was. Definitely.

"Jessica? What are you doing?"

Jessica jumped and turned quickly, surprised by Ally's voice. "You scared me," she said with a gasp, bringing one hand to her chest. "I'm just sweeping up while it's slow."

Ally furrowed her brow and glanced over at Jeremy and Jade's cozy little corner. "You should be using this break to do the time cards, not sweep," she said. "Get Jade to take care of this."

"But—" Jessica started to explain that Jeremy and Jade were just on their break, but Ally disappeared back into her office. Jessica looked over at her so-called friends, laughing over their coffee. She gripped the broom handle with both hands, so hard that her knuckles turned white. And when Jade threw back her head, laughing uncontrollably at something Jeremy had said, Jessica could have reached out and snapped her neck.

Ally's right, she thought, watching as Jade playfully batted Jeremy's arm. *I'm supposed to be the assistant manager. I shouldn't be wasting my time sweeping.* Jeremy leaned closer to Jade, smiling. *That's it,* Jessica thought. *Break's over.*

Girls, Conner thought bitterly as he grabbed his guitar and headed for the garage. *What are they doing anyway? Swapping stories about what a jerk I am?*

He pulled the door at the side entrance to the garage so hard that one of the hinges cracked.

"Nothing works in this place," he spat, slamming it shut even though it sat crooked in its frame. Immediately he plugged his guitar into his amp and turned it up to ten. But when he started strumming, the resulting dissonance of untuned strings and feedback only seemed to scratch the surface of his anger and frustration.

"God, I need a drink," he muttered, removing the strap from his neck and stalking to the back of the garage. His latest discovery had been a bottle of Scotch his mother had stashed in an old cookie jar. Conner removed the ceramic top and grasped the bottle firmly, feeling an immediate sense of relief. As he uncorked the bottle, he forced himself to stop for a minute, absorbing the weight in his hand.

He eyed the dark brown liquid for a moment somberly. "I don't *need* a drink—I *want* a drink," he told himself, letting the words sink in to see how they felt in his mind. He lifted the bottle, letting the light from a back window shine through it, turning the alcohol a brilliant shade of amber. "If I needed it, I'd be like my mother," he reminded himself, already able to feel the warmth of the liquid in his throat. "But that's definitely not the case."

Conner held the Scotch to his nose, letting the peaty smell fill his nostrils. He knew how it would taste, how it would feel. *I'm not like my mother,* he told himself, tipping back the bottle and allowing the warmth to flow into his body. *I just want a drink to unwind. And who wouldn't after this week?* he thought, closing his eyes and breathing deeply through his nose. He paused for a moment, then lifted the bottle again. *Especially since it's only Tuesday.*

Elizabeth Wakefield

<u>Reasons to Give Conner a Second Chance</u>
  The way I feel when he walks into a room
  He has changed his ways for me
  His gorgeous, intense, green eyes
  His perfect lips
  His music
  His writing
  His sense of humor
  I love him
  I think he loves me

        <u>Reasons to Move On</u>
  He kissed Tia
  He might hurt me . . . again

Taking Charge

9

"Jeremy!" Jade squealed. "I swear, you're such a loser." She laughed, throwing back her head again as he smiled yet another sickening, adoring smile.

Jessica approached their table, her mouth set in a grim line. Little did Jade know *she* was going to be the loser tonight. When Jessica was hovering right next to them, Jade finally looked up.

"Jess! You should have heard what Jeremy just said," Jade gushed, wiping away the tears of laughter from the corners of her eyes.

"Here," Jessica said, thrusting the broom at Jade. "You have to finish the sweeping." In an instant Jade's smile vanished and her eyes went flat.

"What?" Jade asked. Jeremy was staring up at Jessica like she had just asked Jade to give her a kidney. But he was just going to have to get over it and realize Jade actually worked here. She wasn't his personal entertainer.

"I need you to finish the sweeping," Jessica said, trying very hard not to look at Jeremy. She had a feeling she wouldn't like what she saw in his expression.

Jade sat forward in her seat and glared up at Jessica. "It wouldn't kill you to throw in a *please*." Jessica felt the heat in her face and knew her cheeks had gone crimson. Okay, so throwing out orders was kind of bitchy, but it was too late now. She couldn't just back down without looking like a total idiot.

"*Please*," Jessica drawled, dragging the word out unnecessarily. Jade stood and snatched the broom out of Jessica's hand, all the while staring at her like she was unable to comprehend such evil.

"Jade, why don't you let me do it?" Jeremy offered, staring past Jessica as if she weren't even there. Jessica could feel his indignation, but it only made her want to lash out at Jade more.

"I asked *Jade* to do it, Jeremy. Not you," she spat, barely recognizing the bitter voice as her own. She knew she was only making things worse, but she couldn't seem to stop herself.

Jeremy's brow furrowed, and he took a small step back, studying Jessica as if he'd never seen her before. "Jess—"

"It's okay, Jeremy," Jade said, holding up one palm. Then she focused a patented snotty look on Jessica and cocked her head. "Jessica *is* my boss," she said. "Besides, my break was just about over anyway."

Jessica smiled smugly at Jeremy, folding her arms across her chest. She tried to ignore the pang in her heart when he just looked away.

"And Jessica?" Jade continued with a perfectly

straight face. "I promise I'll get the broom back to you as soon as I'm done. I wouldn't want you to be without a ride home."

For a moment Jessica couldn't find her voice, but when she heard Jeremy unsuccessfully cover a quick laugh, she recovered and shot him a look.

"Sorry," Jeremy said, casually holding a hand over his mouth.

"Very funny, Jade," Jessica snarled, narrowing her eyes.

"I know," Jade answered with a happy little grin.

Jade started to walk toward the counter, but Jessica got there first and stomped into the stockroom, holding her breath all the way to keep herself from screaming. Once inside, she leaned against the wall and let out a long, slow breath.

Who did Jade think she was? Jessica knew she had been a little bitchy, but that hardly gave Jade the right to make her look like a total witch in front of Jeremy. At least Jeremy knew her well enough to know it wasn't true—right?

Slowly Jessica stepped toward the stockroom door and opened it a crack so she could peek through at Jade and Jeremy. They were still standing by their table, whispering. *Probably about me,* Jessica thought. *As if I care.* Then Jeremy put his hand on Jade's shoulder in a reassuring gesture, and Jessica's heart plummeted.

Apparently she really did care.

*　　*　　*

Tia sat up on her bed and flipped over her pillow. *Oops, guess I already turned it once,* she thought, realizing that both sides were now wet with tears. She stood and walked over to her bureau, pulling a fresh wad of tissues out of the huge box. After using three or four to clean herself up, Tia rested her elbows on her bureau, looking into the large, round mirror above it.

She looked like a train wreck. There were dark circles of mascara under her eyes, and her lids were puffy and red, reminding her of the way Elizabeth's eyes had looked just a few hours earlier. For the ninetieth time she fought the urge to pick up the phone and call Conner, to spill everything to him and just hope all the pieces would fall into place.

But she knew she couldn't do that. What happened between Conner and Elizabeth was up to them now. She was out of the loop. All she could do was hope that Elizabeth was wrong. That Conner would tell Elizabeth she was insane and send her packing.

Tia tossed one of the balled-up tissues at her reflection and turned away from the mirror to survey her room. Used tissues littered the floor, her bed looked like it had been trampled by a herd of elephants, and there was an open container of Ben & Jerry's melting onto her bedside table.

"Looks like my room's having a nervous breakdown too," she said aloud, laughing bitterly at her stupid joke. She stepped over piles of clothes and old magazines and grabbed her garbage can. "What I need is a fresh start," she told herself as she stuffed an empty chocolate-bar wrapper inside.

She walked around the room, picking up all of the tissues she could find, then headed for her night table. Using a pair of old socks she'd never really liked, Tia eased the gooey ice cream container into the trash and threw the socks in on top of it. "Gross," she said. "No wonder I'm losing it. Look where I'm living."

She set the garbage can outside her door, promising herself she'd clean it out later. Then she went back in and snatched the pillows off her bed, throwing them onto the floor. With a quick jump she hopped up onto her bed and started shaking out the blankets so she could arrange them neatly. When she was done, she fluffed the pillows and propped them up against her headboard, pleased by how much cleaner her room already looked.

She was just about to start tackling all of the scattered clothing when something under the bed caught her eye. It was the corner of an old, blue shoe box.

Tia reached under the bed and retrieved it, sighing as she cleared the dust off the top. Slowly she opened it, revealing a picture of her and Angel at his senior prom last year, along with a whole bunch of other photos of the two of them together. Tia flopped down on her bed and flipped through them one by one, smiling at some of the images and feeling like crying when she looked at others.

Finally her eyes settled on one of her, her three younger brothers, and Angel playing at the beach. Angel was buried up to his chin in sand, Tia was feeding him grapes off the stem, and her brothers were all laughing. Tia remembered the day perfectly—the balmy breeze, how much fun they'd all had, and the way Angel had held her chin as he kissed her good night.

All right, she thought, taking in Angel's utterly amazing smile. *Is that how you feel about Conner?* The question made her giggle. *Conner, who used to pee in your parents' flower beds?* Thinking about it now, it was hard to believe that she had actually kissed a guy who had once sat in her kitchen and sampled dog food with her just to see what it tasted like. Then again, her life hadn't exactly been making sense lately.

In a matter of weeks she'd gone from Angel to Trent to Conner to schizo. Suddenly Tia realized that if it hadn't all been happening to her, it really would be laughable.

She closed the shoe box and reached under her bed again, this time pulling out a bright red photo album. It was one that she and Andy had put together when they were only ten. On the cover they had spelled out *The Adventures of the Three Musketeers,* using letters clipped from old magazines, and inside, they had written a story using photographs of the three of them together as illustrations. Tia had to laugh as she went through it, remembering all of the goofy things they had done together. When she reached the end, Tia closed the album and set it next to the blue shoe box.

It was strange. She missed Angel—even more when she saw all the pictures of him—but still, she knew she didn't want him back. It was too complicated. She was ready to move on, to be single, to have some freedom and a little bit of fun—on her own. But when she looked at the pictures of her, Conner, and Andy, she realized there was one thing she did wish she could have back.

Tia stood up and went to the mirror. Conner's picture from junior year was stuck in the bottom-left corner. Tia smiled, remembering how she'd had to force Conner to sign it for her. He hadn't even ordered prints of his school picture, but Tia had managed to snag a proof from the yearbook committee, and then she had badgered him until he gave in and scrawled something on the back. She flipped it over to see his familiar chicken scratch.

Tee—

Friends always.

—Conner

She read it carefully three times, then carefully put the picture back, hoping beyond hope that he had meant it.

"There," Jade said, resting the broom in the corner. "Finished. That wasn't so bad." Jeremy grinned weakly as he broke a new roll of quarters open in the cash-register drawer. She was certainly taking things in stride. Still, being bossed around by one of her friends like that must have stung—even if Jade had held her own against Jessica.

Jeremy cleared his throat when Jade came over to stand next to him. "Hey, look, Jade, if you want to talk or anything . . . ," he offered.

Jade smiled at him, her eyes softening appreciatively. "What? About Jessica?" she asked, lifting her chin toward the back room. "I can handle her. I've known her longer than you have."

"True," Jeremy said, slamming the register drawer shut, but he couldn't help wondering what Jade meant about "handling" Jessica. The last thing he wanted to deal with was more catfights on the job. He knew Jade was new and Jessica was stressed about being the boss, but he wasn't stupid. He knew there was something else bothering Jessica. He just wasn't ready to believe that it was him.

"Hey, I'm going to pour myself some water—you want some?" Jade asked, taking a paper cup from the stack next to the espresso machine.

"Sure. Thanks," Jeremy answered. Jade grabbed another cup and walked to the sink. Jeremy watched as she poured herself a small cup of water and downed it in one gulp, then filled both of them and walked over to him. Ever since her little confrontation with Jessica she'd been a little less alive—like something was weighing her down.

"Here," she said, holding out his cup. Jeremy reached out, letting his fingers brush against hers as he took the cup and once again feeling the incredible electricity that seemed to jump from her body into his every time she was close by. Maybe Jessica was picking up on that too.

But she wouldn't care. She'd made that abundantly clear a number of times.

Jeremy turned to Jade, who was leaning on the counter, staring out the window absently. He moved closer to her and leaned in so his head was just above hers. He tried to follow her sight line, but there wasn't much to see.

"What are you looking at?" he asked, squinting.

"Traffic . . . a couple of pigeons . . ." Jade straightened slightly, her shoulder grazing Jeremy's chest and sending an intense pulse of energy through his body. "Your reflection in the window," Jade finished.

Jeremy refocused his eyes on the plate-glass window and caught her eye. She just stared back at him for a moment, and it was so intense that Jeremy finally had to take a step away.

"Oh," he said, trying to pretend he wasn't nervous about being so close to her, but he knew it was too late for that. Jade smiled and turned around to face him.

"That doesn't bother you, does it?" she asked, her dark eyes bringing out a deep blush in his face. "That I was watching you?"

"No . . . not at all," Jeremy answered, baffled by the fact that he could still speak. Jade never ceased to amaze him. He'd never known anyone like her before. Ever. All he wanted to do was grab her and kiss her, but she was so confident and intimidating, he wasn't even sure he could find the words to ask her out.

But Jeremy had never chickened out of anything in the past. And he wasn't about to start now.

"Uh . . . Jade? I was wondering . . ." Jeremy paused to clear his throat.

"Yeah?" Jade asked, with a grin that told him she knew exactly what was coming.

"Um, would you ever consider—"

Before he could finish his sentence, the door to the back room swung open and Jessica bounced through, looking so perky, no one would ever know she'd been the bitter queen about an hour ago.

"Okay, guys!" she said cheerily. "Time to lock up. Jeremy, Ally needs you in the back. There's some heavy stuff, and she needs a manly man to move it."

Jeremy stepped away from Jade, sure his face was

going to explode from heat. "Oh. Okay," he said, wiping his hands on the back pockets of his jeans. He shot one glance at Jade, who managed to lift one side of her mouth for him, and then he ducked into the back before he could say something stupid.

So much for not chickening out.

TIA RAMIREZ

To: adesmond@stanford.edu
From: tee@swiftnet.com
Time: 7:33 p.m.
Subject: missing you

hey angel—
  what's new at stanford? not much
here except that i've been acting
totally psycho ever since we broke up.
ok, so maybe not psycho exactly, but
definitely crazy—at least, more than
usual.
  anyway, i wanted to tell you that i
think i've figured a few things out
and i'm pretty sure i know how to fix
everything now—that is, if it's not
too late (please don't let it be too
late).
  well, i guess that's it. i hope
things are going well up there for
you (i'm sure they are :-)), and i'll
write you again soon. thanks for
listening.
  love,
  tee

<DELETE MESSAGE>

DOING THE RIGHT THING

10

Conner took a small sip of the Scotch sitting in front of him on the floor and leaned back against the cold cement wall. The bottle was almost empty now, but Conner kept reminding himself that it hadn't been a full bottle to start. *I really didn't have that much,* he thought, aware that his eyeballs were beginning to swim inside their sockets.

His eyelids had begun to feel heavy, but then again, it was getting late. And it had been a long day. He reached over to the boom box on his left and cranked the volume another notch. The band playing on the local college station wasn't one he recognized, but it didn't matter. They were loud, and that was all he was looking for.

Forget Liz, he thought, picturing her sitting at House of Java engrossed in conversation with Tia. *Forget Tia too,* he thought. It seemed pretty obvious what they had been talking about. How could they both just give up on him like that? They were probably sitting there exchanging stories about what a loser he was. Tia could tell Elizabeth about all his past girlfriends, and then Elizabeth could tell her what a jerk he was as a boyfriend.

It must have been fun for them.

He reached for the bottle again and took another swig, but he swallowed it the wrong way and started to cough instead. For a few seconds he thought his eyes were going to burn out of his head as he gasped for air, but it finally subsided. When his windpipe felt clear, Conner's thoughts immediately returned to Elizabeth and Tia. What a joke. They had both claimed to care about him so much, but then he messed up once, and that was it? Conner shook his head. Relationships were so overrated.

Holding the bottle in front of his eyes, Conner examined its contents again. *Brown,* he thought. *Sort of the same color as Tia's eyes.* He thought about the way she had looked waking up next to him. He'd always thought Tia was beautiful. How could he not? He'd just never thought about her in a hookup context because it seemed wrong. Like she was his sister or something.

But she wasn't. And who was to say he had messed up by kissing her anyway? It wasn't like he *owed* anything to Elizabeth. They weren't married. She had no right to expect anything from him. Especially with his unstellar track record.

He'd never even told her he loved her.

Conner stared at the bottle, realizing that there was only one swallow left, and chucked it at the other side of the garage. He watched as the syrupy liquid splattered, bits of broken glass scattering everywhere.

He snickered. It really sucked that every time he came out to the garage, he ended up having to sweep the whole place. Slowly he stood up, steadying himself against the wall. He grabbed the broom and started to round up the debris, herding the bits of dust, dirt, and wet glass together. How had he ever gotten involved in a "serious" relationship in the first place? What was the point? When he had finished sweeping, Conner stared down at the pile, looking through it instead of at it.

Maybe it was time things went back to the way they used to be—a new girl every week. Girls who didn't make him feel pressured just by looking at him. Girls who didn't make him feel things he'd never felt before. Things he wasn't sure he could handle.

Things he definitely wasn't ready to say.

"Jessica." Elizabeth sighed, perking up at the sight of her sister's familiar fuzzy, pink slippers descending the basement stairs. "Finally." She finished one last sentence in her journal, then closed it and hopped off the dryer. "Jess, I'm so glad you're home. I have to tell you what happened when—"

Elizabeth stopped abruptly, watching as Jessica scuffled across the hard, cement floor. She plodded over to Elizabeth and leaned heavily against the washer, folding her arms across her chest with a sigh. "What?" she asked, staring at the floor.

"Hel-lo," Elizabeth said, waving her hand in front of her sister's face. "Rough night?"

Jessica rolled her eyes. "I don't want to talk about it," she muttered, boosting herself onto the washing machine.

Just then the dryer buzzed, and Elizabeth automatically turned around to open it. She felt the warmed clothes to make sure everything was dry, then hauled out a pair of jeans and began folding them.

"Are you sure?" she asked, looking up at her sister. "You seem pretty upset." She set the folded jeans on the table to her right, then reached into the dryer and pulled out two shirts, tossing one of them to her sister.

Jessica caught the shirt and crumpled it into her lap. "Nah," she said. "I've got it covered." She reached over and set the unfolded shirt on the dryer, then lowered herself onto the floor. When she looked at Elizabeth again, there was a bit more life in her eyes. "I want to know what happened when you talked to Conner," she said with a little smirk. "I heard you tell off Tia. Nice job, by the way."

Elizabeth couldn't keep the smile from spreading across her face, but she wiped it away a moment later. "I can't believe I did that," she said, bringing her hand to her forehead.

"No!" Jessica said, grabbing Elizabeth's wrist. "It was good. It was like you were possessed or something."

Elizabeth laughed and turned around to lean back against the dryer. "I think I was," she said, looking at Jessica out of the corner of her eye. She knew Jessica was going to be disappointed by what she was about to say. "I'm not going to do it. Tell him to choose, I mean," she said, staring down at the little hole in her sock.

"What?" Jessica exclaimed. She threw up her hands. "That was like the only good thing that happened all day."

"Jess, calm yourself," Elizabeth said, turning around and grabbing a towel from the dryer. She folded it into perfect thirds and placed it with the jeans. "You know Conner. If I tried to tell him what to do, he'd go ballistic."

Jessica raised her eyebrows as if she was considering the point. "Yeah, I guess he's not the type to take orders from the little woman," she said, leaning next to Elizabeth.

"But I am going to do something," Elizabeth said, pulling out another towel. Her heart was slamming against her rib cage at the thought of saying what she was about to say. She tried to fold the towel, but she suddenly couldn't remember how to do it. She balled it up and tossed it into a laundry basket. Jessica just stared at it like it was going to bite her.

"What?" she asked. "You're going to stop doing your chores?"

"No." Elizabeth laughed nervously. "I'm going to tell him I love him."

Jessica's eyes widened, and her mouth practically dropped to the floor. "You're going to *what?*"

"I know! I know," Elizabeth said, grinning. "You think I'm insane."

"Let me get this straight," Jessica said, leaning one hand on top of the washing machine and gesturing with the other. "Basically you're saying that all a guy has to do to win your devotion is kiss another girl."

Elizabeth reddened. "Well, when you put it that way . . ." She looked into Jessica's eyes and sighed. "He loves me, Jessica," she said. "At least I'm pretty sure he does. And honestly? I think it freaks him out. I mean, he's never even dated anyone for more than two weeks. If you realized you loved someone and it scared you, what would you do?"

A little lightbulb seemed to go off in Jessica's expression, and she smiled appreciatively at Elizabeth. "Run in the other direction," she said slowly. "Like into my best friend's arms." She paused and patted Elizabeth on the back. "Been watching a lot of *Oprah* lately, haven't ya, sis?" she said.

"Maybe," Elizabeth said, picking up the towel again. "I figure if I tell him how I feel—if he knows I'm not scared to say it—maybe he'll chill out about it."

Jessica sighed and grabbed a shirt out of the dryer. "I hope you're right, Liz," she said.

Elizabeth's heart responded with a pained thump. "Me too," she said quietly.

She had to be right. She just had to.

Tia crept into the driveway, keeping low in case anyone was looking out the windows. She was trying to be quiet, but she kept kicking the loose rocks in the driveway with the toe of her canvas sneakers, sending them flying into the bumper of Conner's Mustang.

So much for a career in the FBI, she thought, cringing with every noisy step.

She crouched next to Conner's car and looked up at his window. The lights in his bedroom were on, but she couldn't see him, and there was no way for her to get closer. Suddenly she remembered why she'd never done this before. But maybe . . .

Tia found a small, white pebble and clutched it in her hand, trying to calculate the distance from the driveway to the window screen. She'd never even successfully hit the target for the dunk tank at El Carro's spring carnival, so she was pretty sure she'd never make it. She was juggling the rock back and forth in her hands, trying to come up with an alternate plan, when she heard the faint sound of music coming from the garage.

Tia tiptoed over to the side door and put her ear

up to it. After a minute she heard Conner's voice. He was muttering lyrics along with some band on the radio, and he sounded especially irritated. Tia smiled. Andy was right. There was no way she could ever deal with all of Conner's moods. Not as his *girlfriend*. As a friend, it was different. She could always make a joke out of it or just tell him to get over himself. If she were his girlfriend, she'd have to put up with a lot more or at least be all nice about it.

Tia listened for one more minute to make sure Conner was alone. Then she raised her hand and knocked on the door, simultaneously running through the litany of things she wanted to tell him.

That she still wanted to be his friend, even if Elizabeth had told him not to be. That even though Elizabeth had lost it that afternoon, she was still the best thing that had ever happened to him. That he needed to tell the girl how much he cared about her or he was going to lose her eventually anyway.

She was about to knock again when Conner whipped open the door so abruptly, he made her jump. She was about to open her mouth and start spewing her speech when she actually got a good look at him, and all her ideas vanished from her head. He was wearing faded jeans with the knees ripped out and a tattered plaid oxford. His sleeves were rolled up haphazardly, and the top four buttons were undone, exposing just enough of his chest to draw Tia's attention. She swallowed hard as she tried to look away.

When had he become so irritatingly hot?

"I . . . uh—," she started, noticing that his hair was standing up in the front as if he had combed his hands through it a thousand times in the last five minutes. "What are you—?" Tia stopped, trying to remember why she had come, but the only thing that kept running through her mind was how incredibly sexy he looked. Tired, disheveled, totally spent . . . and *sexy.*

"I—," she tried again, but as Conner moved toward her, her breath fluttered in her chest and left her speechless. Then, in what seemed like slow motion, she watched Conner lean in close, wrapping one arm around her back and pulling her through the door. Tia nearly lost her balance, but his strong arms encircled her, supporting her and lifting her just over the threshold.

He was pressing his lips to hers before she even felt the ground beneath her feet again.

Slowly she moved with him into the cool, musty garage, her body tingling with the sensation of his hands in her hair as they kissed, barely coming up for air. Conner was backing into the room, bringing her with him, and she knew he was heading for the ratty old couch at the far side.

But she didn't stop him. She could barely think. Until he stepped on something and a loud clatter filled the room. Tia ripped herself away, waiting for the fog in her brain to clear. Conner reached out his hand quickly, but she stepped back.

"Wait," she said, glancing around. "What are we doing?" She searched his eyes for a moment, but Conner didn't answer. He just stared back at her with an intensity that was almost overpowering.

When he reached out for her again, she let him touch her. He ran his fingertips along her cheek and under the blanket of her hair. Then he pulled her to him again and kissed her. But this time Tia winced when she tasted his lips. There was something bittersweet. Something she couldn't quite place.

Alcohol? Tia thought as he ran his fingers down her back. *Is he drunk?*

She broke away again and looked into his eyes. They were a little red, but nothing strange. He was probably just stressed and overtired.

"Do you want to stop?" he asked quietly, in a voice that sent shivers running through her.

She just shook her head slightly and let him kiss her again, more gently this time.

He wasn't kissing like someone who couldn't see straight. He was kissing like he meant it, like he wanted her as much as she wanted him. When he started to lower himself down onto the couch, Tia went with him.

He wrapped his arms around her, and she reveled in being so close to him. She knew she shouldn't be doing this. She had moved beyond the point where she could blame it all on Conner. Her entire body wanted him, but there was still some small part of her that felt guilty.

Why did I come over here in the first place? she wondered.

She was on the verge of remembering when Conner leaned her back into the cushions and touched her face almost lovingly. Suddenly nothing else seemed to matter. All of Tia's doubts disappeared, and the only thing she could think about was how right it felt.

She could think about the guilt later.

CONNER MCDERMOTT

12:02 A.M.

I am the biggest idiot in the world. I love Liz. I do. I know I do. Not that she'll ever talk to me again. Not now.

TIA RAMIREZ

12:03 A.M.

ALL WE DID WAS KISS. NOT THAT THAT'S AN EXCUSE. BRUTAL HONESTY? I WOULD HAVE GONE FURTHER, BUT CONNER STOPPED ME. IT FELT RIGHT TO ME. SO RIGHT, I DIDN'T KNOW WHY WE HADN'T DONE IT A LONG TIME AGO.

BUT NOW I'M WONDERING.

WAS HE ACTUALLY DRINKING?

AND WHEN HE TOUCHED MY FACE, WAS HE THINKING OF ME? OR OF LIZ.

ELIZABETH WAKEFIELD

12:05 A.M.

I can't sleep. I can't stop thinking about telling him. How I'm going to do it. When I'm going to do it. Where.

But most of all . . .

Is he just going to laugh in my face?

JESSICA WAKEFIELD

12:15 A.M.

I don't care what happens between Jeremy and Jade.

I don't care what happens between Jeremy and Jade.

I don't care what happens between Jeremy and Jade.

I really, <u>really</u> don't care. . . .

JEREMY AAMES
12:15 A.M.

Jessica doesn't care what happens between me and Jade.

Jessica doesn't care what happens between me and Jade.

Jessica doesn't care what happens between me and Jade.

Do I care that Jessica doesn't care what happens between me and Jade?

Check out the **all-new....**

..... (Sweet Valley Web site—)

www.sweetvalley.com

New Features

Cool Prizes

The **ONLY** official Web site!

Hot Links

(And much more!)

BFYR 232